D0853247

MAY 1 8 2009

LAISH

LAISH

Aharon Appelfeld

Translated from the Hebrew by
ALOMA HALTER

Schocken Books, New York

Translation copyright © 2009 by Aloma Halter

All rights reserved. Published in the United States by Schocken Books, a division of Random House, Inc., New York, and in Canada by Random House of Canada Limited, Toronto.

Schocken Books and colophon are registered trademarks of Random House, Inc.

Originally published in Israel by Keter Publishing House Ltd., Jerusalem, in 2001. Copyright © 2001 by Aharon Appelfeld and Keter Publishing House Ltd.

Library of Congress Cataloging-in-Publication Data
Appelfeld, Aron.
[Layish. English.]
Laish / Aharon Appelfeld ; translated from the Hebrew by Aloma Halter.
p.   cm.
ISBN 978-0-8052-4159-4
I. Halter, Aloma. II. Title.
PJ5054.A755L3913 2009
892.4'36—dc22   2008031755
www.schocken.com
Book design by Robert C. Olsson
Printed in the United States of America
First American Edition
2 4 6 8 9 7 5 3 1

LAISH

1

My name is Laish, and those who like me call me Laishu. I have yet to run into anyone with such a strange name. There are people who are bemused, but most just accept it. I've heard that the name comes from Hungary. Who knows?—my parents died young. A few years ago, I could still see them in a blurred way. Now I'm fifteen, and their features have been effaced from my memory. At times, they'll surprise me in a dream, calling my name. If I ran into them in the street, I wouldn't recognize them. And I, too, must surely have been forgotten by them.

For the past two years I've been helping a man by the name of Fingerhut—a man of middling height, with the look of someone sure of himself. But that's just his outward appearance. He is sick, with an agonizing illness that weakens him relentlessly. I thought that suffering might soften his anger, but I was wrong. His anger, or, actually, his roars, have only become more dreadful over the course of time. If his morning coffee isn't served at precisely six a.m., he's ready to overturn everything. In return for my help, he gives me half a loaf of bread each day and a little milk. On Fridays, there is a piece of chicken with a pickle. If he's in a good mood and he's satisfied with how I serve him, he'll give me more. Once he bought me a bar of halvah. But most days he is immersed in his pain and his anger, and he takes it out on me. I don't answer him. I've learned not to respond. His anger eventually weakens him, and first he falls silent and then he falls asleep.

Once he caught me by surprise, asking me about my name. I told him what people told me. He advised me to change it.

"A name like yours stirs up anger, and people will make fun of you."

"Do you have a name for me?" I asked.

"Why don't you call yourself Shimshon?"

I laughed.

"Why do you laugh? The name will give you strength."

Most of the day Fingerhut lies prone on his wagon, swathed in blankets, writhing in pain. Toward evening he might rally and start talking with those around him. People have no respect for him, but they are still afraid of him. He is a man of means, and many need him.

"Why do you only come begging to me?" he rebukes those who gather around him, driving them away. People do not stand on their pride, and they come back and ask again, both for loans and for charity. Instead of a pawn ticket, he might give a loan, but not outright charity. When anyone asks for financial help, he says, "No one gave me anything."

Fingerhut is very sick, but he never talks about his illness. At one of our resting places, a medic declared that he should go to Vienna for an operation. Since then he hasn't visited a medic. What keeps him going is the power of the hot-water bottles that I prepare for him. When a bottle makes him feel better, he gives me a few pennies.

"Why don't you go see a doctor," grumble the people whose sleep is disturbed by his nightly groans.

"What help will the doctors be?"

"They'll operate on you and they'll give you back your health."

"I don't believe it."

"And what do you believe in?"

This he doesn't answer.

There is never bad without some good. Fingerhut's sickness makes him prescient: he knows what to buy and what to sell, and he always profits. Naturally, he reveals the secret to no one, but I know that this merit comes from his sickness, from his interrupted sleep and constant pains. For nights on end he doesn't sleep. Once he used to be at the center of things, and at night he would terrorize people, but since he fell sick the other dealers keep their distance. His grim face instills terror, and were it not for some thugs, whom he constantly bribes, it is doubtful that people would let him stay on the wagon. And yet he still does not restrain himself: at least once each night he raises himself up, exposes the upper part of his body, and shouts in a grating voice, "Cheats!"

We are a motley crew, making our way along the roads in six wagons. There used to be eight. The wagons are wide, laden with people and all their belongings. There are some remarkably old men and women. The convoy, so they say, is headed toward Jerusalem. I doubt it. There are a few old people who rise early to pray, but most of the others are absorbed by their own affairs and don't have patience for matters of belief.

I get up among the early risers, light a bonfire, and serve Fingerhut a mug of coffee. The morning hours are my best hours of the day. I sit next to the bonfire and sip coffee. As I already said, I don't believe that the convoy intends to reach Jerusalem, even though wherever we arrive, the dealers declare our destination at the top of their lungs. But there can be no doubt about one thing: the name Jerusalem holds great enchantment. When we reach a small town—and most of them are small towns—the locals immediately come out of their squat houses and stand there marveling. Not an hour goes by before the women serve us drinks and sandwiches. In the summer they give us fruit from their gardens. In the cold and the rainy months we sleep in the synagogue. These are the days when fortune smiles upon me. In the synagogue, I always find some quiet, neglected corner where I can stretch out my legs and sleep without being cramped. And the main thing is that I'm given many errands. In return for my services I get a coin or a pretzel. Fingerhut rages at me, saying that I'm neglecting him and threatening to fire me. I've learned how to placate him. At night I bring him a mug of coffee. He smiles, and that's the sign that my wrongdoing has been forgiven.

Once Fingerhut told me that he used to believe that Jerusalem would heal his sickness, but he no longer believes it. The convoy is no more than a fraud. Were it not for the money that people owe him, he would leave it without delay. The opinion of Fingerhut's wagon mates is completely different. They claim that when he joined the convoy he was desperately poor. Over time, he would exploit the weaknesses of his fellow creatures, pretending to be on the committee, ingratiating himself with everyone to get rich. It's true that over the past year he has no longer been pretending, but he remains wicked. If he would help those in need, they would in recompense pray for his recovery, but because he's a miser they ignore him, and he's left to wallow in his sickness.

Once he asked me if I would be prepared to leave with him. I was surprised, and I didn't know what to answer. Finally, I coughed and said that I also wanted to ascend to Jerusalem. I was happy that I said "ascend to," which, by the way, is an expression that people often use. Fingerhut glared at me and said, "Either you're a fool or you're wicked."

"But everyone says we'll ascend to Jerusalem."

"Those words sicken me more than the ulcer."

"My mistake."

"You can steal, you can cheat, but you're not allowed to use those words."

"What should I say?"

"There are words that shouldn't be used. Using them is a fraud. You understand?"

I found it hard to understand him.

Here they quarrel about everything, but not about the deception itself. In the name of Jerusalem we are always welcomed with piety; we are blessed and given charity. This plodding along enables all of us to make a living. Only once, I recall, did a group of furious Jews attack us, driving us away with blows and pitchforks, forcing us to turn off the main road. Entreaties were of no use. They beat the horses in fury, shouting, "You scum! Enough of this mouthing the name of Jerusalem just to bring light to eyes that have lost their glimmer and to turn ordinary folk into generous people."

Fingerhut does not try to hide his thoughts from me, and in the early morning hours, as he sips the coffee that I've made for him, he tells me again and again that this way of proceeding is nothing but a deception, nothing but treading in place. It reflects neither nobility nor the ascent of the soul, but a shameless weltering. His words, spoken early in the morning, are a frightening disclosure of what he really thinks.

"One of these days, they'll throw me off as well," he says, revealing just a bit of his fears to me.

"Why?"

"They always throw off the sick, in the end."

"I'll join you."

"I find that hard to believe."

"I promise you."

"It's not your fault. Man is rotten by nature." He tries to placate me.

From time to time he will say, "Don't leave me."

"I won't."

In return for this promise, he gives me a few candies or a pretzel, but when the black mood is upon him, he leaves no doubt. "You'll abandon me as well." It seems that this is his deepest fear.

One night, one of the old men came up to me, held out a notebook, and said, "In another day I'll be leaving this world, and I want to entrust you with this notebook. I've written in it the names of those who died, and the day of their passing. From tomorrow on, you'll write in it. That's it. Nothing more."

"Grandfather." A tremor escaped from my throat.

"Don't be afraid."

"I don't know how to write."

"It's very simple."

"I'm afraid."

"It's your fate, my son, and you cannot refuse."

"Where should I put the notebook?"

"In the lining of your coat."

"Why did you choose me from all the others, Grandfather?" I trembled.

"That's how it is."

"I'm a thief, Grandfather, and I'm a liar, too."

"Quiet!" The old man raised his voice to me.

I wanted to run away, but my legs were rooted to the spot. I picked up the notebook and slipped it into my coat lining. The old man laid his hand on my head and said, "May the Almighty bless you from His place in heaven." He pushed a coin into my palm and was gone.

The next day I still saw him sitting in his wagon and

praying. He prayed quietly, in a normal voice, like a man who is in no hurry. No sign of bad things clouded his face. I decided that I would return the notebook to him that night. But before I could do it, he passed away, as he had said he would. I hurried to get change for the coin he had given me and added some pennies of my own. The funeral was cold and brisk and without ceremony. After the funeral I distributed the pennies to the poor. The wretched people took them from me without questions and without thanks. One took his share, and with a furious glance said to me, "Where did you get this money, you thief?"

2

Here, everyone's a thief. Even in the summer, people sleep in their coats. If you have a package, you tie it to your body, but even this is no guarantee. Fingerhut, who gives me my daily bread, doesn't trust his heavy coat and sews his money into the shirt next to his body, but they still manage to steal from him. I have no parcels and no money. Whenever I get a few pennies I spend them the same day. Two years ago, one of the old men had a stroke and died after his savings were stolen during the night. Even this tragedy did not put a stop to the stealing. Moreover, sometimes a man may get up and declare, "I went stealing last night." Yet the look on his face is like a drunk who hasn't sobered up. Strange things take place here. Every day I'm astonished anew.

And as for me, since Old Ya'akov gave me that notebook, I find it hard to sleep at night. I don't dare open it. It seems as if the names of the dead recorded in the notebook are asking me to free them from their death. I would take the notebook out from my lining and bury it, if I weren't afraid to.

There have been many times when I've wanted to tell Fingerhut about this. He's indifferent to such disclosures, usually citing the well-known verse *The heavens are the heavens of the*

Lord, but the earth He has given to mankind. It has a frightening meaning: *Don't raise your eyes to the heavens; cast them downward and worry about tomorrow.* Fingerhut's pains have become more intense over the past month, and I'm kept busy for hours preparing hot-water bottles for him. "The hot-water bottles save my life," he says again and again, groaning, and gives me a coin or two.

"Hand out some of your money to those who need it, and things will go better for you. Why do you even need so much money?" People goad him.

"And who's going to support me in Jerusalem?"

"In Jerusalem, God will look after you."

At night, the talk is bitter. The words are removed from their sheaths. Fingerhut refuses to be beholden to anyone. At every hurt he strikes back.

"I'm a bad man, but I'm not self-righteous," he'll say, with a twist of the knife.

"You're rotten through and through."

"What of it?"

Even the intense pains haven't affected his mind. His pains give him strength, if one can say this. Whenever he draws out a word, it's as though it is a poisoned arrow: words like "let's suppose" or "so what?" Tiny words that stoke the fire.

"If you behaved decently, people would love you." They resume their taunts.

"I don't want to be loved," he'll shoot back.

Meanwhile, it's summer and we sleep outside. The small bonfires by the light of the blazing sunset remind me of a different life. Where this life was, I cannot remember.

At times when we stop by a river, the water unexpectedly brings to mind shadows from my childhood. The shadows are very slight, like the light that clings to them. They make me dizzy. I clutch my face with my hands to dull their searing touch.

The long summer evenings that go on deep into the night flood me with longing for my nameless parents. Some of those in the convoy knew them well, but for some reason they haven't told me anything about them. As for me—I don't dare to ask. It is a bond of silence that weighs upon me. My roots are cut off like stumps, and sometimes I feel the pain inside the wounds.

One of the old men told me that at one time my parents also wanted to participate in the journey, but they came down with typhoid and never rose from their sickbeds. After they died, people in the convoy took me in, adopted me, and I've been here ever since. I trust the old men; they're careful about cleanliness and they speak the truth. It's hard for me to understand how they live in this filth. True, people are protective of their honor, but not always. A year ago, for no apparent reason, one of the thugs attacked Old Avraham, hurting him badly. The punishment was not long delayed: typhoid spread through the camp and killed two women.

During the long summer evenings Old Avraham instructs me in the weekly Bible portion. I don't find it easy to study. Old Avraham is a stickler, and if I make a mistake pronouncing a word or I get its meaning wrong, he scolds me. But he doesn't hit me. On Friday mornings he tests me. His tests are also difficult. I have to know the first part of the weekly portion by heart, and if I fail (and I usually do), he rebukes me outright and tells me that I should take my studies far more seriously and not laze around. Otherwise, he says, I'll come to a bad end. I would really like to make him happy, but I cannot overcome my bad memory.

To make me a better person, Old Avraham has given me the task of waking people up in the morning for prayers. It's not pleasant to awaken people from their sleep; they're often angry, and at times they throw things at me. When I complain, he says, "Don't have so much self-pity. This world isn't an amusement park. We must do what life metes out to us without complaining." There's a kind of frightening honesty in his voice, and I find myself submitting to his gaze. Sometimes it seems to me that he hates me, and I would like to ask him why.

After prayers, the old men sit under a tree and study from a book. They swallow the words, and their talk comes only in spurts. It's hard for me to understand what they are talking about, but I love to sit and watch them. Their faces are like skeins of patience. After an hour of study I make coffee for them. I sometimes hear them say, "Laishu is a good boy." It moves me.

After studying, the old men go back to their wagons to doze and I sit, enveloping myself in the morning light and daydreaming of Jerusalem. Among us there's a man by the name of Ya'akov Yitzhak who tells miraculous stories about Jerusalem. It's hard to know if he's a spinner of tall tales or a cheat. In his stories, there are only good people, only the saintly, and miracles seem to happen all the time. Fingerhut hates him and calls him "a cheat, and the son of a cheat." He has lined up witnesses so that Ya'akov Yitzhak will receive not a penny of his inheritance. I also don't like exaggerations. When I picture Jerusalem, it is as a broad, light-filled city—a place where there is no frost or dampness, where a man can lay his head on a stone and fall asleep. I must surely be wrong.

In the winter, there's a sense that the convoy is making progress. At times it seems that our journey is not an illusion— as Fingerhut claims it is—and there is hope that it will come about soon. In the summer we move on lazily, lingering in town squares. The men wander about the villages, trading with zeal; the women go begging; the weak and the sick shake their alms boxes, calling out loudly, "Alms for the pilgrims, alms for the pilgrims! Whoever denies alms to pilgrims will go to hell."

There's a violinist among us, and a flutist, too, and someone who plays the drums. In the evening, after prayers, they play for hours. If there is a wedding in a village they are invited, and all of us are invited along with them. These are hours of wonderful forgetfulness. Afterward, it's very difficult to wake people up for morning prayers, and if the truth be told, only the old men get to prayers on time.

I heard that in the beginning it was very different. Shimon the Righteous was the leader of the convoy. He fixed the times for prayer, for study, and for moving on. Whoever lagged behind would be reprimanded. But since his death the dealers have taken over the convoy, and everyone goes his separate way. True, sometimes the old men rebel, rise up, and try to afflict the money-grubbers; if that proves ineffective, they then declare a fast. Once they fasted from one Sabbath to the next, and forced the dealers to give money to the poor. Their protest was not forgotten, and if the dealers ever have the chance to do something bad to the old men, they do. It has been like this for as long as I can remember.

3

In summer we make sluggish progress, setting up in town squares or alongside streams, trading and getting whatever money we can from people. There are various methods: the women and children move people to pity, the old men pray, and the wagon drivers threaten and cast fear. This three-pronged approach has proved wondrously successful in the past; over the course of time, it has been honed and improved, so now there's a strange kind of coordination among the various methods. Of course we all stand to gain, eventually.

Fingerhut keeps announcing that were it not for his seizures and bouts of weakness, he would not remain here for an extra minute. He says that life for Jews over there is no earthly paradise, but it's not a sham. No one declares morning, noon, and night that he's making a pilgrimage to Jerusalem, and no one aspires to bring redemption to the Jews. For many years, Fingerhut has threatened to abandon the convoy, but he doesn't carry out his threat. Many owe him money, and until they repay their debts, he'll give them no rest. In the evening he gets up, girds his loins, and proceeds to collect his debts. One of the wagon drivers assists him in this loathsome task. Invariably, there is a huge commotion. People scream at him: *Man cannot live by bread alone! There's something higher than us all!*

Widows and orphans shouldn't be threatened! Fingerhut doesn't hold back, but gets right in there and stands his ground, rebuking them outright. He claims that the widows aren't wretched; they keep their savings sewn in their clothes. Loans must be paid back. His successes are not impressive, yet he does manage to retrieve something. I help him sew this money into his shirt, which he never removes from his body.

Though some are even worse than he, people recoil in disgust from Fingerhut, perhaps because sick people usually do not create such an uproar, but curl up in a corner and simply ask for compassion. Fingerhut is audacious in his sickness; he's declared that he intends to die with all his money. What the robbers will do with his money after his death, he doesn't care. This announcement, and others that he comes out with from time to time, are well known by now and have become an exemplar for one and all, but it doesn't stop him. In the past month, his face has taken on a strange determination, and it is clear that he's ready for a long struggle.

Meanwhile, I've overcome my fear and have been reading the notebook that Old Ya'akov entrusted to me. It turns out that it is filled almost to overflowing. At the beginning he wrote: *A List of the Faithful Pilgrims Who Have Died on Their Way to the Land of Israel.* Old Ya'akov made no distinction among people, and he listed them in the order of their deaths. Next to the name of everyone who died he wrote a verse from the Bible, and by his own name he wrote: *God watches over simple people.* In the notebook I found a few things that Shimon the Righteous had said, and things that Old Ya'akov had copied from books. His handwriting is clear and round, and the verses are clearly understandable. I would really like to sit quietly and read, but Fingerhut doesn't let me. He keeps me busy from early morning, preparing his hot-water bottles. Everyone talks about his death, entreating him to give some of his money to the poor, because if he doesn't, the dealers will get their hands on it. These heartless pleas frighten me, but not Fingerhut. He just keeps declaring that it is his intention to recover, collect all the money that people owe him, and live for many years. Every announcement of his attracts shouts of derision. One of the wagon drivers, a vicious man who murdered his wife a long time ago and was imprisoned for years on account of it, joined the convoy after his release at the recommendation of the Holy Man. This sturdy man, whose grimness always terrified me, went up to Fingerhut and asked, "Why are you talking such crap?" Clearly, these were words that he acquired in jail—people here don't speak like that.

"I don't want anything. I'm not asking anyone for anything." Fingerhut raised himself slightly to lean on his forearm.

"Everyone is saying that you should give alms. Why don't you give some out?" He spoke plainly.

"They want my money and I don't want to give it to them. That's it, in a nutshell," Fingerhut sneered at him.

"If everyone says that you should give alms, give them out and don't talk crap. Get it?"

"They're all thieves," said Fingerhut without batting an eyelash.

"What?" he said, his jaw dropping open.

"It's true," said Fingerhut in a clear voice.

The wagon driver apparently did not understand what Fingerhut was saying or perhaps became confused. He came up close to Fingerhut, grabbed his coat, shook him, and said, "Don't you speak like that—you understand?" Fingerhut chuckled, a slight laugh, as if to himself. Ploosh, as he was called, took that as an insult, and again set upon him, this time shaking him hard.

"Why are you shaking me?" Fingerhut asked him coldly.

"Because you're talking crap. Do as you're told to do. Understand?"

"I understand, I understand," and something of Finger-hut's former thin smile played about his lips.

Now Ploosh talked to Fingerhut as the wardens must have spoken to him in prison—abruptly, his words full of hard and bony syllables. "In another place they'd put you in solitary," he concluded.

Fingerhut, to everyone's surprise, opened his eyes wide and gazed at Ploosh with astonishment, as if the person standing over him were not a notorious killer but a wondrous creature.

"Why are you silent?" Ploosh raised his voice.

On hearing this outcry, the wonderment left Fingerhut's face and he closed his eyes.

"Anywhere else, they'd beat the life out of you," Ploosh muttered furiously. Fingerhut did not even react to this. Ploosh turned aside, spitting.

That night, Fingerhut complained of sharp pains in his loins. The hot-water bottles did not ease them, and he asked me to rub his back with witch hazel. I did, and it must have relaxed him, for he fell asleep.

The next day I saw Ploosh sitting on the ground, a man of around sixty eating soup that he had prepared for himself. The dark viciousness that had shrouded his face the previous day hung over him now. People did not try to approach him, and he made no effort to be liked. Most of the day he would just sit on the ground. His years in jail were reflected in all his movements: he found it hard to speak, and his torn words and unclear syllables seemed to emerge from deep within him. The old men tried to draw him into their prayers, but he rarely came. For my part, I didn't dare wake him in the morning. He would be deeply asleep, entangled in his bedding.

Meanwhile, it was a warm and pleasant summer, and people took off their shoes and dipped their feet in the river. In this quiet season the Prut was still swift-flowing, but not as dangerous as it was during other times of the year. This unusual immersion brought to mind a mourning ritual. Perhaps because of the red feet.

In my heart of hearts, I fear the coming days. Fingerhut no longer asks anyone else for help, just me, and whenever I bring him a hot-water bottle or a warm compress, he presses a coin into my palm. He's scarcely eaten in the past few days, and when I ask if I should bring him something to eat, he gives me one of his piercing looks and says, "Don't need it now. What Fingerhut needs now is a little rest. When this pain lets up, he'll be on his feet."

He calls his body "bad flesh" and his legs "pins." When the pains around his loins sharpen, he says: "Ssh, pain! Ssh, you pest!" He once told me, "When someone's healthy, he doesn't even know he's got a body." Now Fingerhut knows each limb of his body.

People no longer come to beg him for alms, and he writhes in pain like a snake. At times he will turn to me and say, "Laishu, you're still young. You're going to see a great many wicked men in this world." In his last days, although he goaded me, he did not make me hate him, even though his wickedness overflowed from him.

He even had bad words for the old men. "They always want to be pure," he said, aiming his poison dart in their direction. Once I found him sitting and staring straight at the corner where Ploosh, who had tormented him, sat. "Strange," he said to me, "I don't hate that thug. I should hate him, shouldn't I?"

Fingerhut died the next morning. I still saw the whisper of that suspicious smile on his pale lips. At his death he was wrapped in a coat, a pillow under his head, and the small bundle of his clothes was tied to his body. There was astonishment, for no one imagined that he would die quietly. In his final days, he had fought fiercely with the Angel of Death. A day before his death he had called out, "Fingerhut will not go quietly! He's got a foothold in this world!"

An hour after he died, the dealers were already picking apart Fingerhut's shirt. There was money in it, but not as much as they had imagined. The dealers had been sure that he had buried his treasure in one of the ditches, but they searched in vain. They cross-examined me as well. I showed them what he had given me and swore I had no more. The funeral was silent, and apart from the words of the prayer book, no one spoke. After the funeral, the poor were given charity. Fingerhut's clothes and his list of those who owed him money were burned. I took the notebook that Old Ya'akov had entrusted to me, and I sat and read through it. Whenever I'm in great pain or feel sorrow coming over me, I draw out the notebook from my lining and read it. As I wrote Fingerhut's name and the day of his death, my hand shook.

4

After every funeral, the wagons are rapidly hitched and we flee the place. That evening the horizon blazed fiery until late. Ploosh drove the horses with a mighty hand, cursed in Romanian, and lashed at their backs in fury. The horses pulled with all their might, but it enraged him that our wagon moved slowly, lagging behind the others.

Toward morning, we reached the village of Shazov. I hurried to wake people for prayers. One of the men, among the more wretched, when awoken from his sleep fixed his blurry gaze on me and exclaimed, "Are you out of your mind?" The others, too, hardly hastened to rise. Ploosh caught hold of me later and said, "Why are you waking people up, you scum?"

Only the old men came to the prayers. They prayed almost silently and without undue emphasis. One of them said Kaddish. The morning light was soft, and it warmed those who were still sleeping. The sun was low, and from a distance the hoarse barking of a dog threatened to break the silence, but not a sound was heard. Everyone's morning sleep was quiet and undisturbed.

After prayers, the old men tossed back a few shots of whiskey and called out together, "A good ascent to the soul and heavenly merit!" As I heard this, I saw Fingerhut's soul, shaped like a transparent bubble, leaving his body and rising to the heavens.

The sun climbed high in the sky, and tall women came out of the low doorways of the houses, bringing us cups of coffee and slices of bread spread with butter. The sight of these tall women brought to my mind a well-ordered life nourished by sturdy trees and water. From my first sight of them, these women amazed me. I loved their calm movements. In the cities, women are short and noisy and never quiet for a moment, and our women are worn to the bone. But country women are full-figured and not embittered.

After the prayers, women and their sick children come for the old men's blessing. The old men close their eyes when they give their blessing. This short ceremony, which lasts only a few minutes, always moves me. Afterward, the women look embarrassed and the children scream. I once saw a mute child, after receiving a blessing from the old men, begin uttering disconnected syllables from his sealed mouth. I've seen many miracles with my own eyes, but I don't like to talk about them.

"One shouldn't talk about miracles," Old Avraham, my teacher, once told me. Since he told me that, I make sure to do as he said.

There was a local woman, stocky and with wild hair, who spoke against the wealthy people of Shazov who neglected the poor, the widows, and the orphans. No one went over to her, and she just stood there, cursing the men and wishing them all kinds of dreadful things.

Much later she was still talking, and two local men approached her and pulled her aside. At first she resisted, calling them all kinds of terrible names, but eventually they took her away as she spoke nonstop, mentioning the names of people and places. But her protests were of no use; the men insisted that she be silent.

The next day she appeared again, even wilder and more

enraged. This time she talked about many things, mentioning names and years, even mentioning the dead rabbi of Shazov. Now the men no longer stood on ceremony with her. They dragged her off by force to somewhere far away. Her shouts echoed in the village, and then suddenly she fell silent, as if her mouth had been sealed.

Angry women appear wherever we set up camp. It seems that just the name "Jerusalem" stirs up words and anger in them, perhaps because they believe that we have the power to right life's wrongs. Whenever he saw women who shouted like that, Fingerhut would raise himself up on his forearm and call out to them, "There are no righteous men and no prophets among us! We're nothing but a rabble of rotten, godforsaken Jews. Harbor no illusions! Do not expect salvation!"

We have a saying, "One mustn't dwell on the memory of the dead." But try as I might to forget him, Fingerhut's face still floats before my eyes almost every day. I recall his gestures so well; they were mostly careless, but whenever he would voice his objections to something, his forearms would appear to stretch and he would seem taller than his actual height. Without being aware of it, I have been taking on some of his gestures.

Tragedies and wanderings have not brought my Torah study to a stop. In addition to the weekly Bible portion and a page from the Talmud, I'm studying the book of Jonah. At this time of the year, Old Avraham is completely immersed in the book of Jonah. Whenever we read a chapter, his eyes light up. But his test at the end of the week frightens me. Why is it only me that he tests? Why do only I have to learn things by heart? Doesn't he see that my knees are buckling from the strain? I've learned that it is forbidden to ask. Complaints and questions annoy old people. They think that the questioner is trying to either contradict or dishonor the sacred texts. Even Old Avraham, an easygoing man, comes down hard on me. He takes me to task over the slightest thing. Fingerhut asked nothing more of me than to get him his morning coffee on time. After he had drunk it, he would light a cigarette and say, "Anyone who steals from a thief should not be punished." And that, if the truth be told, was his entire philosophy in a nutshell.

People no longer mention Fingerhut. His place in the wagon has been taken by a woman named Tzilla. Something terrible must have happened to her, but she refuses to speak of it. Her face is mute, impenetrable, and most of the day she sits in her corner and mends shirts and socks. In exchange for her repairs to their clothing, people give her either a coin or some basic necessities. She neither asks for more nor haggles. Whatever people give her, she accepts without reacting. People say that she is deaf. From others I've heard that she has taken a vow of silence upon herself until we reach Jerusalem. She works from early in the morning. In the evening, she climbs down from the wagon and makes herself vegetable soup. It looks like she was once tall. Her movements are dexterous, without haste or anger. After the meal, she sits without stirring. At times, it seems to me that her gaze is fixed on another place. When I contemplate her muteness, I start believing that the journey to Jerusalem is no fraud. Once a month, I also lay my torn clothes next to her, together with a coin. In the evening the clothes are returned to the same place, mended and folded. I thank her but she doesn't answer me. Everyone in the convoy has a dreadful story or a sickness. People don't speak about the horrors, though sometimes it will show in their faces or seep into some meaningless squabble.

And so we move on. When one of the old men passes away, we quickly bury him in the local graveyard and then hurry along. For the sake of the elderly we should move faster, but laziness and sheer wickedness hold us back. The old men plead and clench their jaws, but the force of wickedness is stronger than everything. I have to admit that these delays are often my own moments of grace. When we stay somewhere for a week or two, I manage to note down the details of the place and the day's events. I no longer fear the notebook. I write, and the Hebrew letters fill me with a zest for life. A proper sentence that emerges from my pen makes me happy for the entire day. The dealers and the wagon drivers do not view this kindly, and whenever they notice me writing, I catch their menacing glances. I write early in the morning, before prayers, or sometimes in the evening, in the woods. A few days ago I wrote the word "mother," and I was instantly terrified by this slip. On the days that no words come, or when my hands are as heavy as lead, I read what Old Ya'akov wrote. His writing is very much to the point, concise and without a superfluous letter.

From leafing through, I learn that Old Ya'akov was seventy when he joined the convoy. His wife was no longer alive, and his sons, traders, begged him not to set out on the pilgrimage. But he ignored them. At first he was certain that it would not be a long journey and that he would reach Jerusalem quickly. But later he learned the hard way that the convoy was not led honestly, and that the wagon drivers and the traders had their own reasons to hold it up. He tried warning the others, but people were afraid. Even his friends, the old men, courageous people, begged him not to provoke the thugs. With great pain and no alternative, he started recording in his notebook what happened to the convoy. He began like this: "Since the death of Shimon the Righteous, the dealers and thugs have taken charge of the convoy. They are crude, insensitive people who neither pray nor study Torah; the only thing that concerns them is their money. I don't know where they want to take us. Day after day, the name 'Jerusalem' is taken in vain. I've decided to write down all our humiliations, so that those who come after us will know how crooked are the ways of man." Elsewhere in the notebook he recorded, "A young person can flee his house when it goes up in flames, but we old folk cannot run away. Taking even small steps means suffering. Every day we bring our slightest gestures and entreaties before God, for Him to do with as He pleases. We have run aground and there's no way out. I wish to warn pilgrims to the Holy Land not to be seduced by those who speak in lofty words. The world is full of scoundrels and people whose only love is money, and the path to Jerusalem has many pitfalls."

Old Ya'akov's insights were very clear. He called Fingerhut "an irredeemably vicious man." In another entry, he was more compassionate and called him "a wicked man who wallows in his own suffering." I find it hard to take leave of Fingerhut's memory, and not only because he used to give me my daily bread. I saw all his dealings, could almost touch them. I say his "dealings," yet I'm not sure that this is the right word. He was of medium height, always wrapped in his cloak, which gave him a clumsy appearance, but his smile was sharp and bitter. More than anything, it revealed that no wrongdoing could be hidden from his eyes. He loathed the self-righteous. His sickness spread through his body and found its way to wound him deep inside. Deeper than he imagined.

5

We left Shazov and encamped on the banks of the River Prut. The Prut was not wide there, but its current was strong and flowed swiftly. The wagons were open, the horses were grazing in the meadow, and people were preparing their dinner. It was a time of day that somewhat lightened the heavy gloom that enveloped our wanderings, because you could see people's faces and the movements of their hands. Their faces were still tense, but preparing the meal calmed them. Even Ploosh, on his knees, was splitting branches for firewood; not a trace of sullenness could be found in his face. The years in prison were no longer visible on him now. He was like an elderly peasant who has been widowed and has no choice but to learn how to prepare his own meals.

Since Fingerhut's death I live without a master. I wake people for prayers, pray, and afterward go to the woods to gather firewood. In exchange for a bunch of twigs, I get two slices of bread spread with oil, or a bowl of soup. In the afternoon I go out to the village to buy provisions for people. People also pay me something for these errands. My teacher, Old Avraham, told me that it is forbidden to go to sleep with money that others might need; to uphold this precept I make sure to check my pockets every evening, and if I have any extra coins, I give them to Blind Menachem. Menachem is a quiet man with few needs; his presence is so insignificant, he is hardly there at all. And yet the wagon drivers plotted to send him away. Indeed, once they even put this scheme into action. Their evildoing cried out to heaven. The old men declared a fast, and the wagon drivers were compelled to go back to collect him. Since then he lives in fear, and his existence has become even more restricted. Whenever anyone approaches him, he trembles.

Menachem was one of the first of those whom the Holy Man gathered about him. He believed that in Jerusalem, Menachem's eyes would be opened. Menachem was about twenty years old at the time. Even now, his sealed eyes retain some youthful characteristics. But over the years, anxiety and fear have left blotches on his face—brownish-yellow stains that distort his appearance. Most of the day he sits quietly, listening attentively. Even at night, he doesn't sleep so much as he naps, half wakeful. At times, when it seems to him that the wagon drivers intend to throw him off his wagon, he shouts out and frightens everyone. He isn't afraid of me. He asks me details about new places we come to, and I tell him. Sometimes he asks me to make him a mug of coffee. Once, when I came to wake him for prayers, he told me how hard it was for him to pray with the old men. I understood him. Prayer doesn't come easily to me, either.

"Pay no attention to the senses, they only lead you astray. The *mitzvos* make a man stand tall." My teacher, Old Avraham, attempts to drum this into me, but try as I might, I find that—may God forgive me—the *mitzvos* weigh heavily on me sometimes. It seems to me that the day will come when these commandments will be canceled and other, nobler ones will replace them.

I love the evening prayers. During them, more so than during any of the other prayers, I sense the presence of my parents, who were cut off from me. For days on end I may not think of them or recall them, but sometimes during the evening prayers they rise from the dead and are pulled toward me, and the barrier between the living and the dead is dissolved. Not that this miracle occurs every evening. On the contrary; at times during the evening prayers a bitter mood descends upon me. It darkens my eyes, and I feel my orphanhood all the more keenly; it is as if my life is not rooted in the world and I want to disappear, just as Fingerhut disappeared into a hole.

"Will we reach Jerusalem one day?" I asked Blind Menachem.

"Of course."

"How do you know?"

"The Holy Man promised me."

True, sometimes his faith can waiver and he can be in the grip of anxiety and fear. Once he woke me up during the night because it seemed to him that the wagon drivers were about to throw him off his wagon. His terror was unfounded. The following day he asked my forgiveness, as if I were a grown man. People often take pity on him, giving him a slice of bread or a bowl of soup. When he's eaten his fill and in good spirits, he describes Jerusalem to me, and a youthful light fills his face.

"What did the Holy Man promise you?" I asked with great foolishness.

"I'm not allowed to speak of it," he said, his face showing his shock. Like all of us here, he, too, has grave secrets. Wicked men sometimes remind him that his elder brothers abandoned him without a penny. He himself never talks about them, but when he hears their names, the blotches on his face redden. The old men draw him into their prayers, and afterward they give him a shot glass of whiskey. On the Sabbath, he's sometimes called up for an aliyah to the Torah. About our Holy Ark and the two Torah scrolls that are jostled about on our wanderings, I'll tell more in due course. The old men are extremely worried about them, and they never leave them unguarded.

As I've already said, in summer our progress is slow, and we seem to be crawling. The wagons are parked in town squares or by the banks of rivers, commerce flourishes, and Jerusalem is forgotten. The old men threaten punishments from heaven but the traders ignore their threats.

And at times—and this will sound strange—the old men themselves cause the delay, out of pure despair. At the beginning of the summer we were in Premishlan, hardly a bustling commercial center. The others wanted to press forward, but it was actually the old men who kept us back. They clung to the memory of the Holy Man of Premishlan and would not budge from the place for several days. The old men sometimes frighten me, for they seem to me like people who are not of this world. But when they open a book and immerse themselves in it, they study the same way young people study. They read a line and interpret it, checking what comes before and what follows; if they find a special word, they immediately ask what could have made the Holy Man put it in just there. Their way of studying, like their prayer, has a kind of forward movement, in the manner of people who are sure of what they think. I want to learn from them, but I don't know how to. My teacher, Old Avraham, is reading *The Path of the Just* with me. He really loves this book. With every line, his face lights up. But for some reason, the words grate on me. Sometimes, when my teacher points to some virtue or other, I feel an uncleanness. And it's clear to me that I will not attain spiritual heights because of the impurity of my body. About the travails of my body I will speak when the time comes, but for now I'll say this: I sometimes bathe in the river, I swim, and I set up a rod and try to fish. In Shazov I reeled in an enormous fish; I brought it to the wagons, where it immediately aroused wonder. The women set to grilling it over the coals and said,

"Laishu is a good lad." At that time of day, the old men were sitting under one of the trees; they looked at us with a piercing gaze, as if we weren't Jews but wild men.

Meanwhile, the month of Tammuz has come to an end. The old men stand alongside the wagons and call on everyone to repent. At this time of year their faces are sunburned and they seem ageless; their eyes are alert and their voices ring out clearly. But their influence here is limited. Only on certain days, or, really, during certain hours on Rosh Hashanah and Yom Kippur, do people listen to them. Nevertheless, they stand alongside the wagons and proclaim what the Torah demands of all of us: "For the Lord your God walks in the midst of your camp, and therefore shall your camp be holy." They repeat this sentence over and over, without getting tired.

Menachem told me that he had been tortured by bad dreams during the night and asked me to take him to prayers.

"What happened?" I try to draw near to him.

"I dreamed that thugs pulled me off the wagon, and I tried with all my might to cling to the boards."

"And could you?"

"No."

"They wouldn't dare to do it." I try to calm his fears.

Menachem revealed to me that over the past year his faith has become weak; without faith, he's in the clutches of bad dreams. Dreams are a person's waste products. When a man is connected to his faith, dreams have no sway over him. His words surprised me.

"How do you know?" I ask.

"That's how I feel."

Apparently, Menachem is not so simple. He takes in everything that goes on around him. His hearing is sharp, and not the slightest detail escapes him. I told him that since the death of Fingerhut my sleep is not what it used to be, either.

"Fingerhut scared me." He revealed a small bit.

"What scared you about him?"

"His laugh. Sometimes he would laugh at night."

That evening Menachem told me that his parents had very much wanted him to marry. They even found him a sighted woman, ten years older than he and wealthy, but he vehemently refused.

"She must have been terrible," I said for some reason.

"I have no idea. It's best that a blind person not marry."

"Why?"

"Because he's blind. The blind are targets for all kinds of brutalities."

"But they have excellent hearing."

"Every day, I tell myself over and over that man has come from the darkness and he will return to the darkness. Life is hard and painful, though we're fortunate that it's short."

There was a kind of chilling clarity in his voice. I was awestruck, and tears welled in my eyes.

6

One morning Ploosh came over to me and said, "You'll be working for me."

I froze on the spot.

"I'll give you what Fingerhut gave you."

"I work for the old men." I tried to save myself.

"Liar."

"I gather and bind firewood for them." I trembled.

"That's not work, that's sheer sloth."

Ploosh drove our wagon, which was hitched to two sturdy horses. The dealers had bought the horses a year ago, and since then Ploosh was our wagon driver. He has no friends and spends most his time with the horses. In summer, when we pitched camp frequently, he worked as a day laborer in fields or gardens. In the evening, when he came back from the fields, he would feed and water the horses, and immediately collapse.

The wagon drivers are creatures unto themselves—people call them thugs. They are tall and sturdy and look like peasants, and each of them has a dreadful history. In any case, our thug is called Ploosh. That appears to have been his nickname in jail. The years of jail are evident in all his ways. He treads heavily and his face is always grim. He loses his temper at the slightest provocation. Most of the day, he doesn't utter a word.

In the evening, before going to sleep, he will mutter a few choked syllables that sound like warnings and then fall asleep. Even his sleep is not like our sleep: he sleeps on his belly, and when he wakes up in the morning, his face is red and covered with wisps of straw. Only the old men draw near to him. He is quiet and submissive in their presence. Sometimes, in the evening, he comes to prayers, answers "amen" to one or two of the blessings, and then takes off. He spends the entire Sabbath sleeping on his pallet. In the morning, he thrusts his hefty right leg out of the bedding, and that is a warning signal not to wake him.

The old men do not call him Ploosh, but Pinchas. When he hears this name, his lips twist into a clumsy smile.

"The new month has come as a blessing upon us." One of the old men approaches him.

Ploosh hastens to his feet, as if the chief jailer has come to reprimand him.

"Wouldn't it be nice if you joined the morning prayers?" The old man speaks pleasantly to him.

"Yes, sir," Ploosh hastens to respond.

"Laish will come to wake you, so don't hit him."

At this comment, his heavy features break into a smile and he lowers his head.

"Laish is an orphan, so he shouldn't be beaten."

"I won't beat him," says Ploosh, without lifting his head.

All the same, I was afraid to wake him up. One of the old men woke him. Ploosh muttered something unintelligible and promised to get up, but he did not.

Not all the wagon drivers are like Ploosh. Among them are some God-fearing men who rise early for prayers. Since Ploosh has taken me to work for him, I've kept my distance, escaping his wrath and trying to stay near the old men. After prayers, I make black coffee for them. They love this drink, and they sip it slowly, singing its praises. I love to listen to their mumblings at this hour. Were it not for my teacher, Old Avraham, who supervises everything I do and instills fear within me, I would spend all my time with them. It seems as though he is always about to reprimand me. Nevertheless, I mustered the courage to tell him that Ploosh had forced me to work for him.

"It's forbidden to work for him," the old man stormed. "You are not allowed to associate with such an ignoramus."

"But he's threatening me."

"It is forbidden to be frightened by human beings."

"He's got his eye on me."

"You must learn to stop being afraid of human beings."

"My teacher, how do I do that?"

"You have to immerse yourself in the river and recite the blessings *He who releases those who are bound* and *He who straightens those who are bent*. These blessings will teach your body not to fear."

I brought my torn clothes to Tzilla and left them next to her. Suddenly she raised her head and looked at me. Until then I hadn't seen her eyes. Her gaze was sharp and went right through me. Her eyes did not leave me for the entire day. In the evening, when I came back to collect my clothes, she looked up, opened her silent mouth, and said, "Laish."

"What?" I was astonished.

"We are near the town where your dear dead mother was born," she revealed.

"I didn't know."

"Your mother and I were in the same isolation ward when we had typhoid," she said, and her face closed at once.

My mouth also froze. This thought, that I once had a mother and that we were now approaching the town where she was born, moved me greatly. I ran to the river and immersed myself in it. I said the verses that my teacher had told me to say. For a long time I sat at the edge of the water, trying to picture the town where my mother was born. I so very much wanted to be near her, to give her some of my bread and to bring her firewood in the evening, but she is far away and no longer in our world. At times, it seems to me that if I would give charity and pray, she'd come to me.

I picture her in death as floating. I know that it's forbidden to think like this, but what can I do? The thoughts or, more accurately, the visions press against my eyes. Whenever I'm sad, I eagerly wait for her to be revealed to me.

We reached Sadagora at night. It's a small town surrounded by tall trees. How did my mother wind up in the north, so far away from this place where she was born? I don't know. I was told that she followed her husband, who was born in Tarnow. Occasionally I get hold of some scrap of information about my parents' lives. The old men are sparing with their words, and I haven't been able to solve this riddle. Yet all the same, somehow I summoned the courage to ask one of the locals if any remnant of my mother's family survived. The man narrowed his eyes.

"What was her name?"

I fell silent, as if I had been caught in flawed speech.

There's a bustling commercial center here. Wagons loaded with flour slowly make their way from the mills toward the heart of the green hillside. At this time of the year, the mills work around the clock, and the smell of flour seeps into every corner. I love the smell; it makes me think of the bakeries along the roads we have traveled.

The old men went to pay their respects at the home of the Holy Man of Sadagora, and I accompanied them. I tag along wherever they go, if only to stay away from Ploosh's watchful eye. When we arrived at the castle, the morning light was at its brightest. Many people were huddled in front of the building, which had been built against an ancient wall. I knew that they were desperate to see the Holy Man. There were people covered with festering wounds, some lacking limbs, and some who grumbled loudly. Here the old men seemed diminished and confused, and they gave alms to the wretched.

"Laishu, you should also give some charity to the needy," one of the old men whispered to me. I approached one of the sick people and held out a coin to him. He immediately took it without thanking me. I was sorry that it had not occurred to me to give alms.

It was the afternoon, and we went to the Holy Man's synagogue. It was a spacious synagogue, and I had never seen anything like it. We went inside rather hesitantly and immediately joined in the afternoon prayers. The high walls threw back our voices with multiple echoes. It was strange that here, of all places, I had a vision of my father and mother as I had never seen them, their hands and feet bound, amid a convoy of prisoners. At the time I had no idea of their fate, but I guessed that there was a secret in their lives. The prayers went on longer than usual, and the longer they lasted, the more I felt that my life was bound up in my parents' secret. On the way back to the wagons, I felt a rush of warm affinity with these streets. The thought that my mother had walked here, that along the way she had come upon the same tall trees that I now saw, the same houses, the same lot in which our wagons were encamped—this thought made me dizzy to the point of tears.

"What are you thinking about, Laishu?" My teacher, Old Avraham, broke into my thoughts.

"I'm thinking about my mother." I didn't hide it from him.

"Where was she born?"

"Here."

"My mother, too," said the old man, and tears glistened in his eyes.

That night Old Yehezkiel died. Though he was very old, he never spoke of death. On the contrary, he had been sure that his strength would see him through, even if the journey was long. He would talk of going to Jerusalem as a man speaks of leaving the town where he lives to go to the town nearby where his forefathers were born.

Whenever one of the old men passes away, I feel my orphanhood much more keenly. Old Yehezkiel was tall and thin. Even as he aged, he did not become stooped. The other old men, even the tall ones, seemed short next to him. When he would pray, he would seem even taller. I was told that his sons showed him great respect; they sewed silver and gold coins into his coat. Although he was apparently not a great scholar, his manner of listening seemed wondrous to me. Whenever the Torah was being either read or interpreted, an expression of deep attentiveness would fill his face.

"Where are you from?" he once asked me offhandedly.

I didn't know what to say.

"And the place you were born, where is it?"

When I didn't answer him, he took a coin from his pocket and said, "Buy yourself a pretzel spread with butter." Since then, whenever he met me he gave me a coin.

"Grandfather," I called to him, and then drew back.

"You should always call me that," he said and hastened toward me.

Since Old Yehezkiel said that to me, I have felt that this wandering convoy is my home, and I do not long for another place. It's true that people's expectations here can be boundless and their threats fearsome, but I, thank God, do not go hungry. From time to time people will say, "Laishu is a good lad, he helps the old men," and I am moved.

But now, after the death of Old Yehezkiel, I feel less bound to these wagons.

7

Everyone in the convoy was at Old Yehezkiel's funeral. He was buried the same day, in a graveyard full of old headstones. In his honor the old men did not allow the locals to wash his body for burial. They bathed and prepared his body for burial with their own hands, and then they carried the stretcher to the mouth of the pit with silent steps.

I have again seen with my own eyes the fiery barrier between the living and the dead, and I swore to myself to do good in the eyes of God, not to daydream or slack off, to pray, and to give charity to Blind Menachem. And like all the other funerals I had attended, this one, too, was without tears. The silence seemed solid; you could have cut it into pieces.

"He didn't make it."

"No, he didn't make it!" the old men railed, their sorrow turning to rage. "If it hadn't been for the thugs, if it hadn't been for the dealers who have delayed the convoy, we would have been in Galacz already." This time they held back nothing.

True, there are some dealers here with wide-ranging business interests, and there are those who have invested their capital in real estate. Even as we travel on, messengers work on their behalf after they have departed and in advance of their arrival. Naturally there are all kinds of shady dealings. Two months ago we were surrounded by gendarmes who would have searched us and made arrests. The dealers immediately went out to meet and bribe them. We were lucky that they were satisfied with what we gave them, and they returned as they had come. There is some justification to the old men's sighs when they say that because of these money-grubbers they will die in darkness, never reaching Jerusalem.

Complaints, I've already learned, are of no use. The compulsion to make money overrides everything. Even a deal that is not all that substantial is enough to make them swerve the wagons off the main road. In their blindness, they assume that they can deceive the old men and confuse them. But how wrong they are! The old men have extraordinary memories, their senses are razor-sharp, and the slightest deviation from the highway rattles them. But they are not able to bring the sturdy horses to a halt. The horses gallop in the direction that the wagon drivers steer them.

"God will not forgive you!" You can hear their fury at night.

On the following day, too, the old men stood in a long line to ask the Holy Man of Sadagora for his blessing. I caught a glimpse of him amid suffering and embittered people, and I was moved. They stood waiting for hours. Toward evening it was clear that only the strong and those who pushed forward would get through the entrance, while the rest would have a long wait. At night the old men returned to the wagons and said their evening prayers in the dejected tones of mourners.

"Do you worry about the time to come?" My teacher, Old Avraham, suddenly turned to me.

I was terrified. "My teacher, what should I be doing?"

"Not neglecting your Torah studies."

I study whenever I get a free hour, but it is hard for me to learn things by heart. If I knew the verses by heart, my teacher would grant me greater favor. But because my memory is not so good, I try to make up for my shortcomings by helping the old men. I chop wood, light bonfires, prepare coffee, and wash dishes.

And despite all this, I could not elude Ploosh's clutches. During the night, while I was curled up on my pallet in the wagon, he came over to me.

"Why are you giving me the slip, you thief?"

"I'm helping the old men."

"If you don't help Ploosh, then Ploosh will throw you off the wagon. You hear me?"

"And who will make the old men coffee after prayers?" I pleaded for my freedom.

"That's not your concern. Starting tomorrow, you're with me."

So that was how the wolf sprang out at me: I knew that my life hung suspended over an abyss, but I didn't imagine that it could just be sloughed off like this. Had Fingerhut been alive, I would have fled to him. Fingerhut had very good connections with the wagon drivers. He would lend them money without receipts and promissory notes, and they respected him for this. But Fingerhut was now in the World of Truth while I was in this world, where the darkness was as high as a wall.

I was too afraid not to obey Ploosh, and the following day found me standing before him. That very day my enslavement began. I worked from the early hours of the morning until darkness. My teacher, Old Avraham, tried to rescue me from Ploosh's clutches, but his entreaty fell on deaf ears.

"He has to work," Ploosh muttered. "There are no free rides."

I thought of running away, joining the beggars, but my dread of Ploosh hovered over me like a whip. I saw how he lashed the horses and I knew that my fate would be no different.

Ploosh worked me relentlessly. Within a week, I learned how to wash down the horses, give them food, water them, and carry a sack of barley on my shoulder. He would punish me immediately for any negligence or mistake. Once he beat me till I bled. When I tried to excuse myself, he called out in rage, "Shut up, you criminal!" and slapped my face. The old men saw my suffering, tried to come to my rescue, and even threatened to declare a fast, but Ploosh, who usually responded to their entreaties, was unyielding. "He must learn how to behave. A few slaps won't harm him."

"You have to be mindful of orphans, they're protected by God," my teacher cried out to him in great despair.

That was how I became a slave in the city where my mother had been born.

Ploosh does not talk to me; he only mutters. If I do not obey his mutterings immediately, he slaps my face and kicks me, but here's the wonder: I've learned to understand his mutterings and do his bidding based on the garbled syllables that emerge from his mouth. At night, I lie on my pallet and ask my mother to save me from this enslavement. Now I see her as a short, thin woman. For some reason, I'm sure that my mother is trying with her entire soul to intercede on my behalf. Her willingness to endanger herself fills me with courage, and I wait with great longing for her to reveal herself. Were she to command me to jump into the Prut, I would jump. Death, after all, would bring me nearer to her.

One night, my teacher, Old Avraham, stole over to me and said, "Laishu, don't despair. God is everywhere, even the deep-

est pit. If you call Him, He'll answer you. He can do anything."
I was happy that he had approached me, and I promised him
that I would be strict in my observance of ritual hand washing
and in praying. On hearing my promise, he blessed me.

The elderly are also suffering. They returned to the Holy
Man's castle many times. I saw them come back at night,
dejected and dispirited, gathering alongside the wagons and
praying softly. On hearing their pleas I also asked God to
shorten the journey and bring us quickly to Jerusalem. Since
my enslavement, I see Jerusalem very differently: as a tall
mountain overhung with thorny foliage, with strong guards at
every point of entry to prevent people from climbing up the
slope.

"Let us ascend the Holy Mountain!" the old men beg.
"Our days on earth are numbered."

"Quiet!" shout the guards, blocking their ears to the cries
for help.

Were it not for my teacher, who comes to me at night, quietly reads to me the weekly Torah portion and a chapter from
The Path of the Just, and imbues me with faith, I would be lost
in my enslavement.

Most of the day we're out plowing. Even the sturdy horses find
it hard to plow this heavy earth. Ploosh works them mercilessly, and if they slack off he vents his rage on them. On the
days when there is no plowing, our work is to transport logs
from the forest to the warehouses, and to deliver sacks from
the granaries to the flour mills.

I find it hard to wake up in the dark, but I do. I rise, water
the horses, and immediately hitch them to the wagon. The

melodies that once ran through my head before the morning prayers, giving me joy, have fled. After work, I sink into sleep as into a deep hole.

I feel my orphanhood all the more in this town where my mother was born. When I complained to my teacher, he rebuked me, "It's forbidden to despair. You have to see this as a test. God tests us just as he tested Avraham, our forefather, and we have to accept these trials with love."

Meanwhile, my life is like that of the beasts with whom I plow. Ploosh lashes them and lashes me with the same whip.

8

While I was being crushed under the unrelenting hand of Ploosh, something dreadful happened. One of the dealers, a quiet one whose existence in the convoy we were hardly aware of, went over to Ploosh and asked him to pay what he owed him. Ploosh mumbled something like "Don't bother me, I'll pay you back." The dealer did not let up but continued making his demands. Ploosh's patience ran out, and he made a movement with his right hand as if to silence him, but the dealer did not budge. He went on presenting his arguments. Ploosh ignored him and turned away. Then the dealer raised his voice and shouted, "It's my money!" Ploosh again made a gesture of dismissal with his hand, grinning to himself.

Even then the dealer wasn't afraid, and he threatened to bring the case before the convoy's committee. If they could not retrieve his debt, then he would go to the authorities.

"Shut your mouth," said Ploosh without turning his head toward him.

"I won't shut up," said the dealer, putting his very life in jeopardy. From up close, he seemed dreadfully thin. He knew that Ploosh wasn't used to being bothered; some of us had even felt the muscles in his forearm. But for some reason the dealer insisted, standing his ground. It was as if he had sworn to himself that fear would possess him no longer.

"Why are you annoying Ploosh?" Ploosh raised his head and addressed him directly.

"I'm not moving from here until you return my money to me." The dealer spoke in a grating voice.

"Ploosh advises you to scram and not drive him crazy." Ploosh spoke in a voice that was restrained, with even a measure of moderation.

"I'm not afraid."

Ploosh must have been astonished by the dealer's lunacy. Perhaps he was afraid to touch this skeleton of a man. In any case, he didn't touch him, but muttered something and became immersed in his work.

It was midday and everyone was busy preparing their meals. The conversation, which hadn't been loud, did not arouse worry. People here quarrel over everything, screaming and cursing.

After a few minutes of silence, the dealer shook himself out of his silence and said, "I won't move from here."

Ploosh did not react to this, either.

Then the dealer poured out a flood of words about the debt. He even stamped his feet. Because he was so short and skinny, he looked like a child who had been denied his demands. That stamping of his feet must have been what set Ploosh off. Without saying a word and without glancing at the dealer, almost as if he didn't quite mean what he was doing, Ploosh went over to the dealer and threw him like one tosses a log onto a pile. He didn't throw him with anger—it didn't even seem that forceful—but the ground was dry and the dealer's body fell heavily upon it.

At first, it seemed as though the dealer was about to get up, because his right leg lifted a little. But it only seemed that way. He let out a braying sound and began to shake. The people nearby rushed over to him. One of the old men knelt down and raised the dealer's head, while another bent over his legs and massaged them. On the ground, the dealer looked even more like a child.

All this time Ploosh stood by his wagon, mumbling in discomfort. But when the tumult began to grow, he sat down under it. People gathered from all the wagons and surrounded the area. The old men spoke to the victim gently, their words sounding like whispers.

The victim didn't react.

"Let him rest," said an old man, wringing his hands.

People stood around for a long time in a kind of frozen intensity that resembled silent prayer. And when this, too, did not help, one of the old men called out loudly that Reb Mordechai would never be forgotten.

"Get up, Reb Mordechai; get up, brother! We're here, eagerly waiting for you!"

The dealer did not react even to this.

The old men took a few steps back and returned to their wagons. The clearing, which had been packed with people, was now filled with emptiness.

One of the dealers brought a blanket and covered the victim. At that moment it looked as if Ploosh was about to climb onto one of the horses and make his getaway. But this, too, only seemed so. Ploosh took a swig from his bottle, lit a cigarette, and did not stir.

Later, two gendarmes arrived.

"Where's the murderer?" they asked.

People made way for them, and they went up to the wagon under which Ploosh was sitting with his legs crossed.

"So it's you," one of the gendarmes said without asking his name. Ploosh got to his feet.

"What's up?" he asked.

As they put the handcuffs on him, Ploosh did not resist. It

was clear that he knew what awaited him and had not been surprised by their arrival. He strode ahead of them, so that they could not hurry him. There was a wild grin on his face, like that of an animal who had given his captors the slip and had then been caught after a hard chase.

The dealer's funeral was held that same evening. The old men washed his body, carried it on a stretcher, and buried the dealer with care. I kept seeing Ploosh's wild smile. It seemed to me that he had joined the funeral procession and was baring his smiling teeth.

After the funeral, one of the dealers tore the clothes of the deceased into strips and distributed his money to one and all. People grabbed whatever they could. It turned out that the dealer had put away quite a tidy sum. He had been engaged in more than just petty trade, and he must have kept some of his dealings a secret. Not even his surname or the name of his hometown was known. They stuck a simple wooden sign on his grave: HERE LIES REB MORDECHAI.

That night the wagon drivers sat around the bonfire. They drank cognac and forced the fiddler to play sad songs for them. The fiddler was a man of around sixty, short and withdrawn. His entire family had been wiped out in a pogrom in his home-town, near Lemberg. He played quietly and with great inten-sity, as if he hadn't been forced to play but was doing it for himself. Before the tragedy, he and his twin brother had been musicians at festive occasions. They were famous not only throughout Galicia, but as far away as Hungary. After the tragedy, he did not play again. He moved to Lemberg and there, with the few who had survived the pogrom, tried to regain a grip on life. He couldn't, but people who remembered his music took pity on him and helped him make ends meet. And the Holy Man, who had been told about his playing, urged him to join the convoy. The Holy Man promised that in Jerusalem his anguish would be healed and that he would eventually be able to play as he once did. The promise came true well before its appointed time. In the convoy, the fiddler found a flutist and a drummer, and they filled him with the will to play again. The three of them would usually appear together, but at the weddings of very poor people he would play alone. Now, too, compelled by the wagon drivers, he played alone.

That night the wagon drivers got drunk. They sang and rambled on until late at night. The old men's entreaties were in vain. Wallowing in their drunkenness, the drivers kept taking swigs from the green bottles. Only toward dawn, after they had cursed the dealers all the way to hell, did they at last collapse into sleep.

9

We left Sadagora the following day. The wagon drivers were sick from their drinking, and they lashed at their horses' backs in fury. We traveled on the dirt roads alongside the Prut. As if by their own accord, the events of the last few days played themselves over in my head. Everyone had witnessed the murder, and yet a mystery hung over the dealer's death. People remembered that he had been depressed before his murder, keeping his distance from even the few who were close to him. Over the past year, successful trading had brought him a tidy profit but his face remained anguished, with a gray pallor, and he chain-smoked. On the day of his death he had been quiet, polite; he had given some clothes to Tzilla and even put in an appearance at morning prayers. He hadn't shown signs of undue anxiety or fear. After prayers, he had gone over to Ploosh; a few people watched as he did so. He had walked as he always did, but death already dwelt within him.

Only after he died did it emerge that no one knew what town the dealer came from, if he was married, if he had any children, or even the reason he had joined the convoy. Others recalled that the Holy Man had decreed that he be permitted to join. If the Holy Man had commanded it, it meant that the dealer was someone who had suffered.

At the first encampment, I brought Blind Menachem a slice of bread spread with oil. He's always forgotten when there is turmoil. I told him of the events of the past few days and how Ploosh had been taken away to jail. He was not happy. His sunken eye sockets registered shock, and his forehead was furrowed. He took in the world through those empty eye sockets, and he could always describe very precise details—a person's height, for example, his shape, to say nothing of his voice. He had this to say about the dead dealer: "He had the voice of a child." Still later, he added, "What a strange death."

Soon after this happened, I became someone else's property. My teacher, Old Avraham, grabbed my forearm, went up to the new wagon driver, and said, "Sruel, I'm entrusting Laishu to you; don't be harsh, and don't mock him. He has to study Torah in the mornings. In the afternoons, he's yours. That's when he can help you. Laishu is an orphan, and the Torah commands us to look after orphans."

Sruel bowed his head, as Christians do, and said, "So be it."

Sruel was a tall, strong man, and his eyes were as clear as a child's. Years earlier, while he was still a young boy, peasants who had been incited attacked his father, beating and injuring him. Sruel, in the garden at the time, saw the danger from afar. Taking his life in his hands, he went to his father's aid. The peasants misjudged Sruel's hidden strength and started attacking him, too. Though he was brought down, Sruel rallied quickly and felled two of the peasants, strangling them to death. His father was saved, and the sentence meted out to Sruel was life imprisonment. He served a full thirty years, and by the time he was released, neither his father nor his mother nor his older brothers were still alive. He joined the convoy a month before the Holy Man died. The Holy Man had noticed him and said, "Why shouldn't he join us? He's a strong Jew."

At first Sruel helped the wagon drivers; later he became a wagon driver himself. The old men liked him and drew him into their prayer group, but he found praying and studying difficult. He said the prayers awkwardly, like someone for whom the words were foreign. When he was called to the Torah, two old men would stand next to him and help him pronounce the blessings. After he was called up, his face would be red and perspiration would bead up on his forehead; he would be embarrassed and mutter incomprehensibly. Once a week, sometimes twice a week, he would get drunk. His drunkenness was not violent and obscenities did not escape his lips, yet there was something frightening about his high spirits. After he got drunk he would wander about among the wagons and call out to anyone standing nearby, "*Lehayim!* Cheers! Jews, you mustn't despair! We'll soon be in Jerusalem!"

Then he would sit on the ground, shouting and singing songs that he had learned in jail. The next day, a bashful Sruel would apologize to the old men and to people in the wagons. For a time the old men tried to insist that he wean himself off alcohol. He would promise, but he could never keep his word. Eventually their demands ceased, since he helped the old men and showed them respect. Apart from this glaring weakness, he was a likeable man whom everyone found easygoing.

Sruel seldom mentioned his years in jail. Once he was asked if he had suffered on account of being Jewish. "No," he replied simply, and a wide smile spread across his face. Even the dealers depended on him, and they would entrust him with their money on the nights when he wasn't drunk. In return for the favor, they would reward him handsomely. Sruel could have become wealthy, he could have left the convoy and built himself a house, but he was deeply bound to the convoy and rooted in its way of life. When he would start drinking, his eyes would shine and he would promise everyone that it would not be long before we reached Jerusalem. There, and only there, would everything that ailed us be healed.

"Who can guarantee that's how it will be?" the dealers occasionally taunted him.

"May God in heaven be my witness." Sruel would raise his hands and blot out his detractors.

His years in jail had not extinguished the childlike brightness from his face, and even when he was annoyed there was still a softness to his lips. Were it not for his drunkenness, people would have loved him unconditionally. Once when he was drunk, he sat on the ground and wept. For some reason, no one went over to him, and he sank even deeper into his tears. I asked my teacher if Sruel was crying about the years that he had spent in jail.

"Not necessarily," he answered. "He's crying over his mother."

"How do we know that?"

"By the tears."

My teacher surprised me with his insight. Because of his closeness to the holy books and to worlds that I will never even glimpse, his perceptions are clear and unmarred by extraneous shadows. I came to appreciate his keen understanding much later. At that time, I just detected a special flavor to his words. Of a cat who stood next to him and fixed its gaze upon him, he said, Cat-Person. There's devotion in his contemplation. He feels close to dogs and gives them signals. I have yet to see a dog bark at him.

"Why are we afraid of dogs?" I asked him once.

"Because there's fear in us."

I obey all his strictures and bathe in the river, saying the verses he instructed me to say. Sometimes it seems that fear is almost extinguished within me. But of course it isn't any more than a momentary ebbing. At night I'm racked by bad dreams, and I wake up shaking in terror.

Last night I saw my mother in a dream. Her face was clear and her eyes stared at me with wonder. I told her that I had been in the town where she was born but that the town had not treated me kindly, and that Ploosh was cruel to me. For some reason, my mother didn't ask for details about his cruelty, but she showed an interest in the fate of the dealer who was murdered. I didn't know how to reply; I was just surprised at her fear. Finally, in a voice that reverberates within me until this very day, she said to me, "Don't worry, my son. I will be with you wherever you go. I am very close to you."

The next day it rained, and we found shelter in one of the sheds in which the summer grain had been stored. When the owner of the shed heard that we were on a pilgrimage to Jerusalem, he crossed himself and said, "You can stay here as long as you want to. Anyone on his way to Jerusalem is blessed." I was greatly moved on that rainy day. The thought that my mother was so near to me relieved my heart of some of the anguish that had weighed on me like a stone. I lit a bonfire and prepared some soup for Menachem and myself.

10

The rain prevented us from pressing on and kept us imprisoned under the awning. The nights filled with screams: again the thieves were stealing whatever came to hand. The old men were more vulnerable than anyone else. They stood alongside the dark wagons, their nightshirts covering their nakedness, and were silent. Years ago they also would have shouted, but now, if truth be told, there was nothing left to steal. Even so, people steal from them, too.

"Robber!"

"Sodom and Gomorrah!"

The shouts were useless; anyone used to stealing was hardly going to stop. Those who were caught admitted it, but they would not return what they had taken.

Not every night was so desolate. There were nights when a pleasant sort of hominess enveloped us. The bonfires burned softly and the aroma of coffee seeped into every corner. Man did not hate his fellow man, but raised his eyes with brotherly love and a measure of compassion. In these rare hours of grace the dealers would hand out charity, the wagon drivers did not torture their helpers, and from every wagon a small shot glass of liquor would emerge. Such a time of grace occurred two years ago. One of the dealers, a violent and compulsive man who had cast fear even upon the thugs, suddenly became drunk, ripped open the lining of his coat, and started handing his gold out to every outstretched hand. He was a man whose business dealings had extended as far as Hungary, but he had never once given charity. The old men refused to accept anything from him, because one doesn't accept charity from a drunk. The man pleaded and promised to drink no more. Eventually the old men consented, on the condition that he wouldn't be stingy and would give charity to those who needed it. The dealer accepted their terms and swore his allegiance; the old men acquiesced and accepted his money.

After he had distributed the gold, there was a marked change in his behavior. He confined himself to his wagon and severed all ties with those who had worked with him or for him. At first this seemed to be a ploy, but it quickly became evident that the man had really changed. Since then, he has lived a withdrawn and detached life; he neither troubles another living soul nor is troubled by one. Everyone calls him the Gold Man. The thieves don't steal from him, and those who are in the same wondrous state treat him kindly, as if he were suffering.

Still, he does not come to morning prayers. A few of the old men tried to persuade him, but though he listened to their words with his head lowered, he did not obey them. They eventually stopped bothering him about this. He would spend most of his time stretched out in his wagon, or sitting cross-legged. I heard people say that his soul was in the clutches of a dank humor and that he didn't have the willpower to pull himself out of it. Others told me that he abandoned his father years ago in one of the hospices, and though he promised to come back to look after him, he never kept his word. It must have weighed upon him; the day he learned that his father had passed away, he opened the lining of his coat with its store of treasure and distributed his money to one and all. It's hard to know the truth. The man doesn't speak, and there is no one who knows him. Sometimes, as he rises to his feet, some of his former arrogance returns. This must be an illusion: he has changed, and it is doubtful that any amount of wandering can restore him to what he once was.

Over time, his wagon became a meeting place. Sometimes you would hear in the camp: *Let's meet this evening by the Gold Man.* Ploosh did not like him and would mock him, but the Gold Man would only clench his jaw and bear the ignominy in silence.

Sometimes I want to give him a handful of firewood, but something stops me. You never know how a silent man will react. One evening, without any warning, he went up to poor, wretched Tzilla and began to berate her. It was hard to know what he was talking about. At first she did not react, but as he stood there, ticking off a list of her misdeeds, she burst into tears. People put him in his place, and he was silenced. Since then, his silence has deepened. I have already noticed that there is a hidden bond among silent people, mainly a bond of resentment. This resentment is not to be found amid those who speak freely. I have learned that there can be violent people among the silent. When their silence overwhelms them, they burst out. Beware of those who are too silent, the old men warn, and there's truth in their words.

Sruel is good to me. He has already told me a bit about his life in jail, and every evening he tells me more. At times he sounds as though he is still amid murderers. "Even among criminals there can be decent people," he reveals to me. I believe him. When he is drunk, he speaks with enthusiasm and shouts, *"Hear O Israel, the Lord our God, the Lord is one."* He promises that the journey to Jerusalem will not be drawn out and that we will soon gaze upon the face of the Messiah. One evening, in his drunkenness, he surprised me by turning to me and saying, "So we'll be friends, won't we?"

I was frightened. "I will do everything you tell me to do," I said.

"Don't be afraid, Laishu. We'll overcome all the setbacks and together we'll reach Jerusalem."

At that moment Sruel did not seem like a drunk to me, but like a Jew who had forgotten his learning.

That night he told me that in his jail they would beat the prisoners every day, on the days when they rioted and on the days when they didn't riot. The prisoners would also hit one another. Jews did usually not end up there. Once a Jew arrived who had lost his mind along the way. The man kept muttering, "I'm in big trouble, I'm in big trouble." He lasted a week and then passed away.

Our wagon drivers have been in tough jails, punished with solitary confinement and strokes of the lash; it was there that their mutterings and sullen expressions became part of them. They take their anger out mostly on animals, but people also do not escape their clutches. When someone in the camp is not to their liking, they play tricks on him and mock him, and even beat him. Sruel is different from the other wagon drivers, not in his outward appearance and not in some of the mannerisms that they all share, but in the timbre of his voice. There is a light in his face, and something of its softness is transferred to the animals he looks after. The horses love him and obey his commands. Apart from the horses, he has two German shepherds and a falcon that eats out of his hand and sleeps with him. The falcon circles around us most of the day, always high in the sky and always alone. In the evening it lands upon Sruel's shoulder. Sruel feeds it scraps of chicken that he has saved. The sight of the falcon is not really pleasant, but on Sruel's hand or on his shoulder at least it's not frightening. When it lands, it shakes its head with a look of happiness.

Sruel's love for animals does not cloud his love for human beings. If he has a spare loaf of bread or sack of sugar he will give it to the needy. If someone is in need of a bandage or even some charity, he won't hesitate to turn to Sruel. Sruel is never stingy, and when he is drunk, the generosity of his heart knows no bounds.

11

The distance from Sadagora to Czernowitz is an hour's travel, but heavy rains and disputes delayed us, and we arrived in Czernowitz two weeks later. The old men have little affection for large towns and cities, and whenever we approach one their faces tense and anxiety clouds their eyes. Not so the ex-convicts and the dealers—they appear much happier and become quite animated. Big cities seem to energize them, filling them with daring. I saw how they were in Lemberg, where we spent several weeks. There they were like devils, trading whatever they could lay their hands on. In the city they are generous spendthrifts, stuffing banknotes into the old men's pockets. After a day of fervid trading they tire from their efforts and make their way to the gaiety of the taverns. Toward morning, they return to the wagons with flushed faces and clothes that reek of cognac and tobacco.

The old men sigh whenever the dealers return from their nightly debauchery. "God Almighty, see in whose clutches we find ourselves!"

In Czernowitz we halted the wagons in an abandoned square, not far from the Street of the Jews. Our trio—the fiddler, the flutist, and the drummer—burst into wedding songs and old melodies, and a goodly crowd immediately gathered around them. The committee passed around the large copper bowl, and our herald, Reb Pinchas, announced in a strong, deep voice, "Give charity generously to pilgrims. Safeguard for yourselves a place in the world to come." Reb Pinchas is a Jew who is far from easy to size up. He rises early for morning prayers and he is close to the old men, yet all the same he is not quite as he seems. I have often seen him getting drunk with the wagon drivers. But there is one matter on which everyone concurs: he's an excellent herald, and he has brought it to a fine art. He is not a whining type of herald; on the contrary, his bearing is proud and erect, and he declares in a forthright way that our pilgrimage is important and vital. If, with God's help, we should reach Jerusalem, every Jew will reap the benefit. Apart from being our herald, he also enacts in the square the story of Joseph being sold into slavery. Effortlessly changing clothes, Pinchas plays all the parts. As Joseph, he speaks in a youthful and flowery voice; when he is the patriarch Jacob, his voice is old and feeble. Joseph's brothers speak in deep voices, like peasants. The performances last a full hour, and sometimes even longer. Everyone applauds and fills the bowl with coins. Once Reb Pinchas had a bitter argument with the committee. He claimed that apart from his regular salary, he deserved to get a percentage of what is received from his performances. They rejected his claim: it would be either a regular salary or a percentage. I have seen his performance dozens of times. He always either adds something or takes something away. It's never the same.

As I've said, in the city all of us are filled with vitality, except for the old men. They know that the business dealings will turn people's heads, that their good qualities will get corrupted, and that only a disaster will save the convoy from ruin.

Now that I am no longer tyrannized by Ploosh, my teacher has become stricter with me. After prayers and after I serve the coffee, we sit and study the weekly Torah portion. Old

Avraham tries to keep me away from the sights of the city and to instill within me a love of the Hebrew letters. But it really is hopeless; when I'm in the city, I fall under the sway of the dealers. They keep me rushing about from place to place. When my errands have been successful, they give me an extra banknote. Like the rest of them, I could have sewn my savings into my coat, but my teacher will not allow that. And once, when I summoned up the courage and said, "Well, everyone sews money into their coats," he threw me a piercing glance and said, "Not from bread alone do we live." Since he said that to me, I am careful never to go to bed with as much as a penny in my pocket. Before going to sleep, I go over to Blind Menachem and empty my pockets. Sometimes I would like to leave a few coins for myself, but this is a fleeting regret, and the transfer is swift and quickly forgotten.

Czernowitz is a big city, and its lights burn throughout the night. Between errands, I steal away downtown and drift about the streets. They are clean and shiny, and beautiful women proudly stroll along them. If I have a coin in my pocket, I go into one of the cafés and spend some time there.

"Where were you?" My teacher greets me anxiously.

"I was doing errands." I hide the truth.

"So late?"

He immediately takes a holy book out from his coat lining and starts to read it with me. It is important that I see the Hebrew letters before I go to sleep. Hebrew letters can redeem; they have the power of a heavenly sign that induces pure sleep.

"Pure sleep protects the purity of the body, so a man cannot be so easily led astray," my teacher whispers into my ear. He's right. Since our arrival in Czernowitz, my sleep has been troubled. Young girls draw me to them with enchanted skeins, and the dealers joyfully brag that it doesn't count if someone steals from a thief. Sleep weakens me, and I wake up with pounding headaches.

But strange dreams do not ravage my sleep every night. Once in a dream I saw a young girl. She was tall and beautiful and she said, "Your name is Laishu, isn't it?"

"Yes, how did you know?"

"That's how it seemed to me. I'm not wrong, am I?"

"You're right, my name is Laishu."

"I've been looking for you for a long time."

"How come?"

"My mother told me long ago that there's a youth in these parts whose name is Laishu. She said it would be easy to find him, for only he has such a name, and I, for some reason, didn't believe her."

My voice was strained. "My name is Laishu—you really can believe me."

"If that's how it is, then I'll ask my mother's forgiveness," she said and disappeared.

She had been so close to me that I marveled at how she managed to slip away.

After morning prayers, I serve each old man a mug of coffee. At this time of day, a purity envelops the faces of the old men. They hardly speak, but the few words that emerge have warmth and clarity, and I pray that these moments will linger forever.

At night, mothers bring their ailing children. There are also the sick, the deaf, amputees, and grown children from whose throats come angry, birdlike sounds. The old men greet them alongside their wagons, converse a bit, and then bless them with fervor. I have seen the power of the old men on several occasions. In Czernowitz they wrought miracles, pure and simple. Everyone respects the old men and lavishes tremendous amounts of love on them. But we don't know how to honor them properly, we don't heed them, and we secretly mock them. In vain they shout, "Renounce your ways, you wayward children!"

In the convoy, this falls on deaf ears.

12

Congealed within us there is a deep secret, a secret that I have concealed so far. In a structure resembling a birdcage but built to the height of an average person, a young girl named Mamshe has been shut away for years. She is thin and depressed, and her eyes are sunk deep in their sockets. Most of the day she is curled up soundlessly on the pallet in the cage, but there are days when she sits cross-legged and stares vacantly. At night, mostly on summer nights, she gets up on her knees and screams like a wounded animal. Everyone is chilled by her wretched existence. It is impossible to calm her down. Her screams can go on for hours; sometimes it gets even worse. Three women and a wagon driver now take care of her; when necessary, another wagon driver helps them.

Mamshe was brought to the Holy Man a month before his death, wild and injured from bites she has given herself. Then and there, the Holy Man decreed that she be taken in. Because she was already imprisoned in a cage, they hoisted it up onto a wagon and covered it with a blanket; she's been wandering around with us ever since.

As I've said, at first no one could bear her screams, but the Holy Man held firm: she must not be taken back to the town where she was born. He warned us to treat her gently, and to speak to her as one speaks to an ordinary person, as if she understood everything that was said to her. Her hands were to be tied only when there was no alternative. The Holy Man's injunctions are not always heeded: the women who take care of her say that they sometimes have to slap Mamshe's face.

There are also times when she stands quietly, her large eyes radiating an immense, painful sorrow, and you see quite clearly that she has been tortured by evil spirits since childhood. God alone knows why. At such a time, one of the women may go over to her and try to talk to her. It's useless. The prisoner will throw her a piercing look, as if to say, *Why are you disturbing me?,* and immediately turn her back and curl up in her bedding.

Mamshe's screams used to be even more spine-chilling. But they've found different ways to calm her, including drugs, which make her slightly more docile. During the summer nights, from deep inside her thin body, voices emerge that send shock waves throughout our camp.

They have often been on the point of opening Mamshe's cage and letting her go, but whenever they were about to do it, something went wrong or they suddenly had pangs of remorse, and so she was not released. In Czernowitz, there was a marked change in the intensity of her screams. They cut through the air like a saw. Even back in Sadagora, Mamshe had pounced upon the two women who were washing her, biting and scratching them. At the time, the thinking was that this was just an isolated outburst, but in the days that followed it was clear that she had changed. Her screams grew more and more piercing.

The people who took her side tried to defend her. "She'll calm down, she always calms down eventually," they said. But this time the majority did not support them, and their arguments carried weight. They claimed that her screams would draw the gendarmes, who would certainly waste no time conducting a search and confiscating merchandise, to say nothing of ready cash and who knew what else.

In a final effort to take care of Mamshe, a doctor was brought in. The doctor, a short, bald Jew with a thin smile that played about his lower lip, tried to examine her with the help of two wagon drivers. She writhed in their hands and was eventually tied up. The results of the examination were not surprising: she was mad and there was nothing to be done.

"I'll give her tranquilizers," said the doctor. But the medicine also proved useless. Moreover, her shouts became even more spine-chilling. A few old men stood by the cage and pleaded with her, promising that if she would stop shouting, they would not only remove the rope from around her hands but would also bring to her every day the sweet gruel that she so loved. But no amount of coaxing worked. Her screams were like cries of pure terror.

Eventually, there was no choice: it was decided to release her. That evening, two wagon drivers opened the cage. At the sight of the open door and the light that spilled inside, she withdrew and huddled in a corner, let out a few trembling sobs, and covered her head with her blanket.

"Get out, Mamshe, get out!" The wagon drivers raised their voices. On hearing their shouts, her body trembled and she curled up even more. "Get out!" they kept shouting. Even these shouts could not make her budge. She gripped the bars with both hands. Then they inserted a long pole into the cage. The pole touched her loins, and she got up onto her knees. The tip of the pole must have hurt her, because suddenly, almost as if she had been burned, she dashed out and ran under one of the awnings. The wagon drivers chased after her, but she escaped toward the reeds on the banks of the Prut.

All night people expected her to return. It appeared as though she was hiding in the undergrowth and eavesdropping. The bonfires blazed and people prepared supper, but great anxiety lurked everywhere. The cage stood open next to the wagon that had carried her. She did not return. And neither did she return the following day. A few old men went over to the reeds and called out, "Mamshe! Mamshe!" There was no response.

The wagon driver whose wagon had carried the cage, who had suffered from Mamshe's screams and had harbored an implacable hatred for her, was now walking about looking very angry. Her disappearance had unsettled him, and it was he who turned to Sruel and asked, "Can't you ask the falcon to find her?"

"Don't know how to talk to him," said Sruel, in the manner of a peasant.

The previous year a woman had disappeared, one of the quiet ones, and no one knew where she went. For a long time they searched for her in the villages. The dealers bribed the gendarmes and village elders, and they looked for her in barns and ditches. Finally, it was the falcon that discovered her. He circled above, marking the place. To our great sorrow, that was how we found her—quite lifeless.

"You don't speak to the falcon?" the wagon driver asked Sruel again.

"No."

"So how does he understand you?"

"I don't know."

"Falcons get along with people?"

"The first time I saw it was two years ago. I held out my hand and it came to me."

"Do you call to it?"

"No."

"It comes to you by itself?"

"It always finds me. If I'm in the camp, it comes to me in the camp. If I'm out in the fields, it comes to me in the fields."

"Strange, isn't it?"

"Why?"

"Falcons don't usually form attachments to human beings."

"What can I do?"

13

Mamshe's disappearance cast a shadow over the day. We spoke of her with veiled regret. People wondered how she could be managing all alone among the desolate reeds. They were now convinced that she had understood everything that had happened over the last few days, and that she had not been able to bear her shame. That was why she kept shouting, *Mamshe! Mamshe!,* which means little mommy. Her shouts at the start of our journey later became her nickname. We had no idea how much a part of us she had been. Her face, red from the welts she carved with her own fingernails; her body, curled up on the floor of the cage; her emaciated legs, which she exposed whenever she went berserk—her entire being clung to us now.

This time, too, the dealers acted as they always do when there's an emergency: they paid two retired gendarmes to search for her. For several days the gendarmes wandered about the reeds and eventually returned empty-handed. For some reason, we were now sure that the river had swept her away. This thought was particularly painful, because she was afraid of the water. There were of course the coolheaded dealers who claimed that it was not necessary to get excited. A crazed creature has its own life and one shouldn't get mixed up in its craziness; it doesn't think as we do. Perhaps she was fine in the reeds.

"This is not a Jewish way to speak." The old men silenced them. "We are commanded to be compassionate."

For several days Mamshe's disappearance hovered over the camp and covered everything we did with silence. Although Reb Pinchas continued with his performances he, too, fell prey to a deep melancholy. Even the wagon drivers, who were used to getting drunk after a day's work, did not drink to excess and did not let lewd words come out of their mouths. But the urge to trade must be stronger than all else, and in the big city this compulsion was borne on the wings of imagination. From Czernowitz the roads lead to Vienna and to Lemberg; if you turn off into the railway station, you can buy and sell and turn a profit all at once. In Czernowitz, I saw how the dealers were entranced by their imaginations, how luck favored them, and how they soared. But I also saw how they fell, and I saw the pits that they dug for themselves with their own hands.

I, too, benefit from the turmoil: my pockets are full of coins, some of which I stash away. My teacher, Old Avraham, undergoes torments because I spend most of the day outside the camp and not studying.

"A life without Torah is wretched," he drums into me whenever he encounters me. It's strange, but I don't feel this way. I work for the dealers and share in their big secrets. I smuggle herbs and cash in my pockets. It's highly dangerous, but I have learned to enjoy it. The dealers draw me close, and at night I sit with them, drinking coffee and listening to their exploits. When I am in their company, trading seems like a colorful gambling arena. I find it more spellbinding with every passing moment. I sink into a sleep full of dangers, and I survive.

One night, intoxicated with success, the dealers took me to a nightclub called Lily. As soon as anyone enters, he is given an alcove, a woman, and a bottle of liquor. A heavy pall of cigarette smoke hung over the nightclub. I was given a woman who was not tall and who spoke a German that I understood, with a ring to it that I found pleasant.

"Where are you from, my dear?" She addressed me in a friendly tone. I recognized the phrase "my dear," even though it had never before been spoken to me.

"I live with the wanderers." I revealed a bit to her.

"Wonderful," she said, "for it means that you are a free man. And where are you headed?"

"We're traveling toward the sea."

She asked and I answered her. I immediately noticed that two of her side teeth were missing, which lent a sort of beauty to her face. Sometimes a defect only accentuates beauty, as with our Gitel, of whom I will say more in due course. She did not tell me anything about herself, and I did not dare to ask. I was enchanted and dumbstruck. My dreams had come true, but I felt my hands were completely numb, my tongue babbled incoherently, and whatever came out of my mouth was ridiculous.

"And are you Jewish?" She surprised me.

"Yes." I laughed.

"Me, too."

That astonished me; she did not look Jewish.

"The Jews are better, aren't they?"

I didn't know what to answer, so I said, "The Jews are very successful."

"True," she said. "You've got it."

From what the dealers said, I knew that these women were worse than snakes, that they cheat you and steal right from your pocket. I did not have a thing, and whatever pennies I had, I gave her immediately. She glanced at them and said, "These coins will shine on Maya's luck. She will look after them and not spend them lightly. Not every day does such a sweet lad come to Maya. She only gets the predators, not the cubs. The cubs are soft and good."

I had never before heard such words. There are women in our convoy, but they are embittered, without any charm, and they cast heaviness and gloom on your heart. Sometimes I would hide so I could watch them washing themselves. It was intriguing but ugly. Now I understood why the dealers said that a man should take a woman from among the non-Jews. A non-Jewish woman is a woman; our women only spread gloom and bitterness. Maya, if I can believe her, is a Jewess, but she has no traits that are noticeably Jewish.

"How long have you been here?" I asked. My question greatly amused her. She grabbed my head, kissed me on the lips, and said, "Tonight Maya is going to ruin this cute one. It is a shame to ruin him, but there's no choice—he must be ruined. What's your name? Laish? I've never heard a name like it. Who gave you such a name?"

"I don't know."

"You don't know?" she said, and laughter flushed her face.

She was already drunk, but she continued to drink. I had heard from dealers that these women lie and that you mustn't believe them. But I, for some reason, believed her. She told me that the Prince of Holstein was courting her and had asked for her hand, but that he was a predator. All predators were scum; only the cubs were good.

Suddenly she turned to me and said, "Even this cub will forget Maya."

"I won't forget you."

"Stick out your tongue," she demanded. "Your tongue is pink. That's a sign that you're healthy and that there's nothing wrong with your heart."

Then she fell silent. She was cross-eyed, and the powder on her cheeks was cracked. When at last she roused herself, she muttered, "Cubs must be strong, you hear?"

"What?"

"Why don't you talk?"

I became afraid. "What should I say?"

"You're not a golem, you're not made of wood. Say something!"

"You're very beautiful," I said.

"That's not what they say," she replied with childish pique and a chuckle.

Then she took a compact and lipstick out of her handbag and made up her face. I wanted to say something to her, but I couldn't come up with a word.

When she finished putting on her makeup, she poured herself another glass of liquor and cursed the Prince of Holstein. Deep lines suddenly appeared on her face, but this didn't make her look menacing. I wanted to tell her about Sruel's falcon, which perches on his lap and sleeps there at night, but I wasn't sure that she would like that. Eventually I said, "Czernowitz is a very pleasant city." I had heard the word "pleasant" from one of the wagon drivers and found it to my liking.

"What's so pleasant about this city?" she asked crossly.

"The streets," I said, for some reason.

"The streets are ugly because the people are ugly, if you know what I mean. In this city, everything's ugly. They're all predators. Look at this," she said, and swiftly pulled up her dress. Her thigh was notched with two pink scars. "And you say that this city is lovely."

Then she fell silent and it seemed that she was about to leave me. I wanted to take her hand and kiss it, but I was afraid to.

"Maya," I said.

"What do you want, my dear?" she said distractedly.

"Our Sruel has a falcon."

"What are you talking about?" she said.

"Every night it lands on his shoulder. They're good friends."

"Did you say 'falcon'?"

"Yes, a falcon."

"That's impossible."

"I swear to you."

Again she laughed aloud and said, "'*Falcon, falcon from the skies. . . .*' Falcons keep their distance from human beings, don't they?"

"The falcon really loves Sruel."

"What are you talking about, my dear?"

"Sruel feeds it scraps of chicken."

"What a marvel!"

Much later, when she was thoroughly drunk, she grabbed me with both hands and said loudly that she would never forget me.

"Now we'll slowly take off the cub's shirt, and we'll envelop him in lots of love. Cubs need warmth and love. The predators must be driven away without mercy. Isn't that so?"

We returned very late. The dealers were drunk and lighthearted, and one of them, Salo—about whom I'll be saying more later—clung to me and kept repeating one sentence, as if striking a stone: "What a magnificent evening, what an unforgettable evening." The rest of them straggled along the streets, singing old songs, throwing stones into the puddles, and cursing. When we arrived at the wagons, the light of the last watch had already flickered out. I was tired and blurry, and I collapsed like a sack.

14

The following day I didn't awaken on time and I didn't rouse the men for prayers. The old men were angry at me, and I made an effort to placate them with something special: I bought some poppy seed cakes and I quickly prepared coffee. At the sight of the coffee and the fresh little cakes their eyes lit up and my negligence was forgiven.

Maya stayed with me. I envisioned her standing next to the wagons, and whenever she was asked what she wanted, she would burst out laughing. Her laughter, a laugh that had become coarsened by the cognac, echoed in my head wherever I turned. But when she mumbled, "My cub has fur that's as soft as silk," her voice was like that of a young girl. Eventually, and by now in quite a fog, she forced me to swear that I would never forget her. I swore. She looked at me and was about to say something, but instead of words, vomit spurted from her mouth. She doubled over, sinking to her knees. I helped her clean the carpet, and she asked me not to tell anyone about it. This last request of hers, which was made when she was completely sober, I remember clearly; it was as if she had entrusted me with her innermost secret. Then there was a tumult in the corridor as the dealers emerged from its recesses, and one of them, whose voice I recognized immediately, called out in a wild, licentious way, "Where's Laishu? Where is he?"

"I'm leaving; I must go," I said.

"You're going?" she said, and for a moment her gaze rested on my face.

At noon we were told that Ploosh was being held in Czernowitz's central jail, and that four o'clock was the visiting hour. This violent and frightening man, whose years in jail were indelibly marked on his face and his clothes, who had terrorized people and animals alike, who had killed two people and who knows what other dreadful things he had done—this man now stirred a strange pity within us.

The dealers lost no time. They put a bowl on the ground and cried out in a loud voice, "For the ransom of hostages!" Reb Pinchas refused to act as the herald. He argued that a Jewish murderer falls outside the category of hostages, and because his lot must be with the murderers with whom he will be judged, he deserves no pity. Even the old men were divided on this: some claimed that Ploosh should not be abandoned, while others insisted that one had to ignore him, that a murderer must be thought of as dead.

My teacher, Old Avraham, was one of those who went to visit Ploosh, and I accompanied him. A great crowd had gathered around the jail. The swarthy faces of the peasants revealed both the weariness and the dullness of the oppressed. The four of us—two of our dealers whose names I didn't know, my teacher, and myself—stood among the crowd of peasants; the longer we stayed there, the more something of their heavy muteness clung to us.

When the doors would still not open, a groundswell of anger arose from the peasants. The sentries, who stood in the watchtowers, countered with a wild roar, and the peasants fell silent. When at last they opened the doors, everyone pressed inside into a narrow yard that had tall, narrow railings. One had to wait in line to get in, but, as usual, the strong ones pushed ahead and they got in first. It was already night when we entered the visitors' room.

"Talk," said the guard. "You've got twenty minutes."

My teacher turned to him. "How are you? We've brought you a few necessities." The dealers laid the two packages we had brought with us on the counter. The guard checked them and said, "Take this one."

"Well done," said Ploosh, lowering his head.

"How is it here?" asked my teacher.

"Not that bad." The familiar brutal smile spread across Ploosh's face. He did not look wretched.

"Are there other Jews here?" my teacher asked.

"No," Ploosh replied, and his smile broadened.

"And what do you do?"

"I clean the yard."

"Do you need anything?"

"No."

"We'll be moving on soon."

"Where to?"

"Who knows?"

"And who's going to drive my wagon?"

"Sruel."

Ploosh's eyes immediately narrowed, as if he were about to grab a bull by its horns.

"He has no idea how to treat the horses!" he said with barely restrained fury.

"How do you mean?"

"He doesn't treat them right!"

"We'll see that he does." My teacher tried to soothe him.

"I wouldn't put the horses into his care. They are good horses and have to be taken care of right. He hasn't a clue about horses. Understand?" Ploosh's poorly contained anger flushed onto his face, and it was clear that this man had not a single living soul in the world apart from the two horses whom he humbled with a mighty hand. Now even they had been taken from him and given over to a man whom he hated with every fiber of his being.

"You can't hand such good horses over to that scum!" he roared. On these kinds of visits, my teacher would usually try to whisper some words of Torah in the prisoner's ear, but when he saw Ploosh's fury, he could not.

"May God have mercy," he said, without looking Ploosh in the eye.

"I don't know what they want of me," said Ploosh, and covered his face with both his hands, as if he had forgotten the reason he was sitting here.

"May God have mercy," my teacher repeated.

On hearing these familiar words, the smile crept back onto Ploosh's face. It was that same wild smile of his, though now somewhat pursed.

"We must be going," said my teacher.

"Go in peace," said Ploosh, and seemed happy that this blessing had rolled off his tongue.

The roads were already dark, and we made our way slowly, as if we had been rebuked. Ploosh's fury thundered in our ears for a long time. When we approached the wagons, one of the dealers asked my teacher, "Why does he hate Sruel?"

"I don't know," said my teacher.

"Everyone knows that Sruel is a good man."

"I don't know," he repeated, but it clearly preoccupied him, too.

It was the time of day when the musicians were deeply involved in their playing. They played slowly, and with great devotion. At first I immersed myself in the unassuming sounds made by our flutist. The music lightened my heart, easing my memory of what I saw at the jail. For some reason it seemed to me that from now on my life would be different, that different lights would surround me, and that I would be one of the tall, strong ones, with no fear of what the future held. Should it become necessary, I would go forth to protect those who were weaker, because the Children of Israel were descendants of angels, and it behooved me to act with courage and generosity, as befitted the children of angels. A sensation of being in Eden filled my soul, making me unable to stir until the musicians had ceased playing.

But that night I was tortured by dreams. I dreamed that Ploosh had been freed from his chains and had returned to our wagon. Sruel was unable to escape from his vengeful hands and was badly beaten. No one came to his aid. I also tried to run away, but Ploosh had cunningly surrounded the forecourt with high, narrow railings that he had brought with him from the jail. I awoke from the nightmare happy that I was free and that I would soon light the bonfire, fill the pot, and prepare coffee for the old men.

15

My life has changed beyond all recognition. I feel joined to
Maya, and this bond fills me with hidden joy. It seems to me
that the errands I run are for her sake alone, and that someday
I will be able to bring her many kinds of cosmetics and lots of
silk stockings—but how will I find her? The dealers are intoxicated with their commerce. They transport contraband in
broad wagons that are hitched to three Belgian horses. Money
is passed from hand to hand, and in the evening it is sewn into
coats. The old men see this and weep with rage. But their
anger makes no difference. It cannot pull the dealers out of
their feverishness. The musicians, too, are awake until the
small hours, and the way they play together has greatly
improved. Jews in Czernowitz are generous and fill the bowl
with banknotes and coins. Reb Pinchas has come to an understanding with the dealers; now he appears twice a day and
occasionally does a midnight performance as well. The story of
Joseph being sold into slavery is a huge success. The big yard is
surrounded by a fence, and tickets are sold at the entrance. Reb
Pinchas is now assisted by two actors, and the large expanse
looks like a real theater. Blind Menachem plays the patriarch
Jacob, sitting on a large chair and silently taking in all the bad
news. Lame Yekutiel is lowered into a pit, which has been dug

especially for the performance. His voice, which rises from inside the pit, is strong and shocking. Although he is begging for his life, his pleadings are neither tearful nor wheedling; they have the force of a strong man who has been taken captive and is trying to free himself from his fetters.

After midnight, when the commotion has subsided, the old men get to their feet and shout, "There is no forgiveness for money-grubbers who delay our pilgrimage to the Land of Israel. The God of Israel will not forgive you for worshipping silver and gold, or for delaying our souls' redemption and twisting the straight into the winding. The God of Israel, who knows a man's heart and his innermost thoughts, He and no other will bring you to trial." As they say this, the old men are like the ancient priests who were taken captive and exiled.

I hoard every penny so that I can go back to visit Maya, but my savings are not sufficient. Last night I stole from Blind Menachem's coat. I did it quickly, dexterously, and he did not feel it. The following day he sat and wept like a child. I swore to myself that I would never steal from him again and that I would return what I did steal sevenfold. But even this theft was not enough for me. I continued to steal until I had the necessary sum.

As darkness fell, I reached the nightclub.

"Who would you like tonight?" said the woman at the counter.

"I'd like Maya."

"Maya no longer works for us."

"Why?" I said loudly, which must have astonished her.

"Because she didn't serve our customers as she should have, and every night she would cause a scandal."

"So she isn't here?"

"Not with us. We can live without her. A woman who doesn't know how to guard her honor, a woman who vomits, this sort of woman does not deserve to be here with us."

To me it seemed that those were not words that issued from her mouth so much as sparks of fire, and that she was using those sparks to lash Maya's back.

"She didn't vomit," I said, and I was happy I said it.

"That's a lie; she vomits every night. A woman who doesn't know how to hold her liquor shouldn't come here. We don't force any woman to come here. Certainly, a person may have a drink or two, and even get a little tipsy, but vomiting— that's disgusting! It's not professional."

"So she won't be here anymore?" I asked loudly, and it sounded foolish even to me.

"She won't cross this threshold while I'm here."

"That's a pity," I said.

"We have, thank God, interesting women here, women who have studied at high school."

I wanted to say something to her, but the words stuck in my throat.

"I don't know what a young man sees in her," she threw after me.

It was night, and a damp mist trawled along the city's broad sidewalks. People streamed downtown and I was swept along with them, as though I had been condemned to an aimless life.

When I returned to the wagons, my teacher, Old Avraham, came over to me. He was not harsh with me this time. He spoke of what was happening to the old men who had been placed in the hands of the dealers and the wagon drivers, and of their steadily dwindling hopes. There was neither anger nor resentment in his voice, only a quiet anguish for which there could be no consolation. I wanted to offer some comfort, but in my heart I knew that empty consolation, like a vain oath, is forbidden.

That night, dreadful screams rent the darkness and

awakened people from their sleep with a start. The screams were short and sharp, and they came from the direction of the river. We were certain that they were the despairing screams of Mamshe, pleading for help. The entire camp was aghast. Some of the dealers lit their lanterns and plunged into the reeds. The reeds looked higher now than they did in the daylight.

"Mamshe, don't be afraid," they called from every quarter. Some of the men beat a path to the banks of the Prut, waving their lanterns and shouting, "Where are you, Mamshe? We won't do anything to you. You have nothing to fear. We won't imprison you in the cage."

For a long time they shouted in a variety of different voices, but no answer came. The night was quiet and a fine mist hovered above the waters of the Prut.

Then a fight broke out between two of the wagon drivers, and shouts and threats could be heard.

"I'll cut you up into little pieces, like a butcher!" one of the men shouted in a voice that made the camp shudder. "Exactly like a butcher!"

Hearing these shouts and the threats, the old men came running and stood between the opponents.

"It is forbidden to speak like this! Jews don't speak like this!" They would not move until there was calm and the warring factions had returned to their wagons.

It was hard for me to fall asleep that night. I decided to return the money I stole from Blind Menachem. I doubled the amount, and I shoved it inside his pocket. The following day the sockets of his blind eyes lit up. He was as happy as a child and told everyone that the money had been returned to him. Then he called out in sheer joy, "The Children of Israel are the sons of angels! Let no one fault them."

16

In Czernowitz we were joined by two elderly men. No one was happy about it, not even our herald, Reb Pinchas, who seemed to take fresh delight in every new acquaintance. They procured two places on one of the wagons and showed the committee members that they had enough cash for the expenses of the journey. Our old men warned them straightaway that there were people who stole during the night and that they should sew their money into their coats. They were tall, elderly men and, as it happened, they were cousins. Their long coats looked well on them, and their expressions spoke of honesty and calmness of mind.

Old Avraham, my teacher, did not hide from them that the journey was by no means smooth, that there were quarrels and delays, and that we would sometimes stay in one place for weeks on end. The elderly men listened but asked few questions. The parcels at their feet were well packed, but I saw right away how the thieves would loosen them and rob the men of anything they could. I was moved by compassion for them.

One of them did ask about the cage. When they heard the story, their eyes opened wide.

"One supposes that is how it has to be," they said rather

naively. They had lived in a village not far from Czernowitz. Their wives had died many years before and their children were scattered in all directions. Until a month ago, they still worked by themselves in their orchards and kitchen gardens. Then, after harvesting their plums, they decided to sell their property and set off on a pilgrimage to Jerusalem.

They were honest village folk, and their faces attested to this. When people warned them that there were thefts at night, they smiled as if they had been told a tall tale.

"Jews who have been given the Torah do not steal," one of them said.

"They do steal, for our sins, and how they steal!"

Not even after the first robbery did their naïveté vanish. They fought with the thief and thrashed him. No clouds of doubt or fear darkened their clear faces. They prayed, studied Torah, and in the afternoon they washed their clothes in the river. When one of the thieves came to them and returned what he had stolen, they did not forgive him or pretend to be offended or wretched.

"Stealing is a crime. Even goyim have learned not to steal," they said without equivocation.

"But what can I do?" the thief asked. "My hands steal all by themselves."

"Hit your hands; you must have no pity upon them."

"I do hit them, but it doesn't help."

"Just keep God in front of you, for He is the Judge of the World."

"How?"

"Recite aloud: God commands me not to steal."

Country Jews constantly surprise me. Their way of believing is different from ours. They observe the commandments simply, and they give what they should to those in need. They do not lean toward sophistry and they do not exaggerate. There is a kind of clarity in what they do. Our old men love them and are devoted to them, as if they have qualities that the old men themselves do not possess.

"What's your melody for 'Magen Avos'?" I heard one of our old men ask them. The old men question them closely about prayers and the rites of ritual immersion. In the Carpathian Mountains, the ancient traditions of the followers of the Ba'al Shem Tov have been preserved, traditions that in other places have been forgotten or become muddled. I loved them and the way they would listen and talk. They loathed thieves, and they called compulsive thieves "immoral destroyers." There were compulsive thieves in our convoy who could steal with tremendous skill. Were it not for their own pangs of remorse, they could have been enormously rich. They could be easily swayed, returning either the entire haul or what remained of it. I would occasionally find them sitting and weeping by the banks of the river.

I got to know one of them, Itcheh Meir, very well. He would sometimes make me a gift of a banknote or some coins and order me to immediately buy myself a meal at the corner store. Once he came over to me and said with the seriousness of a teacher, "Take this coin and buy yourself a package of halvah; don't delay, do it quickly." He had perfected the act of theft to a degree that no one in the convoy could approach. He must have been around fifty, and he seemed to have earned his livelihood from stealing since he was a child. He came to the Holy Man asking to be healed of this compulsion, and the Holy Man told him to join the convoy. On joining, Itcheh Meir immediately announced that he was a thief and that people should be on their guard against him. He stole that very first night. He was never caught in the act. Afterward, he would admit what he had done and return everything he had stolen, or some of it.

More than once it was decided to banish him from the convoy, which would have been easy enough. He was neither strong nor the kind of person to make a huge fuss. But all the same, he wasn't driven away. Among the dealers, from whom he would mainly steal, there were those who admired him and swore by the magic of his artistry.

When they would ask him how he did it, Itcheh Meir would answer, "I don't do anything; it's just my fingers. They're the pimps for my crime." On hearing this reply, everyone would laugh. But it was, apparently, the honest truth.

Sometimes one of the wagon drivers would attack Itcheh Meir and start beating him. Everyone would immediately rush to his defense, explaining that it was not from malice on his part, but compulsion. It is hard to satisfy the wagon drivers. Eventually they left him alone, but they would grumble and curse him and his weakness.

The old men loved Itcheh Meir because he liked to learn. He knew entire portions of the Torah by heart. He particularly loved *The Ethics of the Fathers,* and at every opportunity he would cite verses from it. On the Sabbath he would pray with great piety, but as soon as the Sabbath was over, Itcheh Meir's fingers itched for cigarettes and thievery. Occasionally, he would boast that he had never been caught and that his hiding places had never been discovered. The truth was that this wasn't so much boastfulness as a kind of wonderment at all that had happened to him. When he would return what he had stolen, a smile would spread across his face—the clear smile of a child. It was hard to be angry with him, to condemn him, or to give him a thrashing. Even the strictest of us did not consider his thefts a crime.

In Czernowitz one of the dealers betrayed him, and that night two gendarmes came to lock him away. As he was being handcuffed, the old men together went over to the gendarmes.

"Good sirs, there must be some mistake," my teacher said to them. "This is a convoy of pilgrims. We are bound for Jerusalem, and there are no thieves or criminals among us. We are all intent on just one thing: reaching the holy city as swiftly as we can, to pray and to beg for mercy on behalf of all God's creatures."

The gendarmes were impressed by the old men's bearing and by my teacher's words. They immediately released Itcheh Meir from the handcuffs and stood as if rebuked. And when he offered them a bottle of liquor, they refused to accept it, since one doesn't accept gifts from pilgrims. Everyone was satisfied with what my teacher had said and was happy that Itcheh Meir had been spared. But for some reason my teacher became sad; he curled up in his corner and refused to utter a sound.

17

Two weeks in Czernowitz, and the heat of commerce had not subsided. The old men were furious and threatened to declare a fast. The dealers tried to placate them by promising that they would trade no more and buy only the necessities vital for our journey. The moment they were ready and the wagons set up, we would be off.

The old men didn't believe them and demanded that we set out immediately. They said that if we did not, they would declare a fast and call all the Jews of Czernowitz to see the extent of the fraud with their own eyes. In the meantime, to placate the old men, the dealers distributed free loaves of bread, vegetables, and fresh fruit. On the Sabbath eve, two cooks prepared a Sabbath meal for the whole convoy. There was no trading, everyone ate to his heart's content, and even the bitter women could not complain.

"Czernowitz is a beautiful city; its Jews are rich. So what if we put aside a little money? Even in Jerusalem, one will have to make a living."

In this way, the dealers tried to win people over.

. . .

Ya'akov Yitzhak, the man who used to tell tall tales about Jerusalem and the graves of the righteous, has ceased doing this. The dealers now have him completely under their thumb, and he has also become money-crazy. Like everyone else, he sews whatever he earns into his coat, and it swells from day to day. A grin of foolish self-satisfaction is spread across his face. The little charm that he once had is all but gone. He has become completely submissive and seems lacking a will of his own; he does whatever the dealers tell him to do. Fingerhut used to harbor an implacable hatred for him, but everyone else would lend an ear to his yarns. Now his soul has been emptied of all its imagining. I find its hollowness terrifying, and I'm apparently not the only one. Sometimes the old men talk to him and coax him to come to prayers. Until recently, he observed all the commandments, but he was always impressionable, like an overgrown child. Now there is no light in his face. He has adopted some of the dealers' gestures and their perfunctory way of speaking, but not their happiness. A pensive bewilderment extends across his forehead.

"So, how will it be in Jerusalem?" the wagon drivers taunt him.

"Why are you asking me?"

"Once you used to tell us stories about Jerusalem. Have you forgotten?"

At that, he runs away from the wagon drivers and cozies up to the dealers. But the dealers do not treat him with respect, and he looks like a man who is hunted, whose pursuers will soon overtake him.

That evening I set off for the street called the Street of the Jews. Maya was sitting on the steps of an abandoned building, taking swigs from a bottle and uttering incomprehensible words. I was afraid to approach her. If anyone tried to come near her, she would throw him one of her drunken glances and curse him. I was about to suggest that she join our convoy. I rehearsed what I was going to say: *Our convoy is quite unique. We are on a pilgrimage to Jerusalem.* But the angry way in which she was sitting put me off, and just as I was about to go over to her, the words vanished from my mouth. There are days when she is quiet, when people don't bother her and she takes slow swigs from the bottle. It's strange; she's more frightening on these days. Finally, I summoned the courage and went over to her.

"I'm Laish," I said. "Perhaps you remember me."

"Who are you?" She fixed me with a scornful gaze.

"My name is Laish, and I would like to invite you to join our convoy."

"What are you chattering about?"

"Our convoy is encamped quite near here. If you wish to, you can join us."

"What convoy are you talking about?"

"Our convoy, which is making a pilgrimage to Jerusalem."

"Get out of the way. I've already heard these excuses."

"Our convoy is a good convoy."

"And what will you give me?" She suddenly embarrassed me.

"I'll be your helper."

She laughed a drunken laugh and wiped her face with her sleeve.

"Move aside," she said without looking at me.

"I'll willingly move," I said, placing at her feet a bottle of cognac that I had brought with me. Apparently, she had not expected this tribute. She smiled and said, "The child has given me a bottle of cognac."

Again I invited her to join our convoy. My words must have irritated her, for she raised her voice and shouted, "Get out of here! Beat it!"

After that, I wandered around the streets for several hours. When I returned to the convoy, the night was already dark and dense. People slept in their wagons and some dozed next to the flickering bonfires. The wagon drivers sat near the reeds, drinking and singing and imitating the lowing of the beasts. I tried to slip away from them, but this time I was not so lucky.

"Laish, come here! What have you been up to outside so late?"

"I took a walk."

"Tell that to the old men. Show us your pockets."

I took all my coins out of my pockets and showed them.

"You shouldn't be hoarding money in your pockets," said one of the wagon drivers, and snatched it all away.

"That's all the money I have."

"Work, and you'll have more."

I knew that all this had befallen me because I had not been careful about prayer. Since I saw Maya, my thoughts have been distracted. There were also my thefts—another black mark against me—and although I had returned what I had stolen from Blind Menachem, that did not absolve me of punishment. By the way, since Menachem has been appearing in Reb Pinchas's performances, he has changed. Before each one, Reb Pinchas drums into him that he has to be quiet and pleasant and not get excited, and that he must receive any bad tidings without panic, since the great virtue of our forefather Jacob was his tranquillity. Reb Pinchas says that everyone is deceitful, everyone lies and slanders others, but our forefather Jacob was not overly hasty in his judgments because he knew that lies would be proven false and that the truth would come to light. Menachem's blind countenance absorbs it all, and he does as he is told. And the next morning, in the light of day, his face reflects a spark of the nobility that his performance had bestowed upon him.

18

On the Ninth of Av we were still in Czernowitz. Toward evening, at the proper time, the old men prepared sackcloth and ashes, low stools and wax candles. Their faces were downcast and their white foreheads mournful. The fast of the Ninth of Av is a hard fast, perhaps because the skies are clear at this time of year, the trees are in full bloom, and gusts of wind carry the scent of blossoms; this hardly brings thoughts of disaster to a person's mind. But, wonder of wonders, on the eve of the Ninth of Av, the clear horizon suddenly changed, and it became even grayer than the dejected twilight that surrounded it. The old men wasted no time and immediately began chanting from the book of Lamentations.

It was like this every year, but this fast was clouded by an argument between the dealers and the old men. The old men said their lamentations quietly, but from the very silence a searing pain burst forth: *Why are you cheating us? Why are you delaying us? Why do you leave us to die in the darkness of Exile?* The dealers apparently sensed this great silent cry, and they sat dejected, with lowered heads.

As the mourning grew more oppressive, long, drawn-out sobs burst forth from the reeds. They made the camp shudder.

We immediately recognized Mamshe's voice. That was how she used to cry out when her wrists would be handcuffed so she could be taken to the toilet or to be bathed. They were the yelps of a wounded animal.

Everyone hurried to the reeds, fanning out around them. Barely a few moments had passed when a terrifying sight revealed itself. In a puddle of mud, sunk onto her knees, sat Mamshe; her face was deeply scratched and blood flowed from her bare arms.

"What happened, Mamshe?" people asked as they approached her.

"They killed me, they killed me," she muttered audibly.

"What did they do to you? Tell us. Don't be afraid."

"They killed me," she muttered again.

The women pulled her up from the puddle and brought her to the wagons. She was wearing the same stained night-gown that we all recognized, her feet were bare, and she was taller than the women who had grabbed her. Gesturing with her thin arms, she tried to explain what had happened to her. The women washed her, served her soup, and offered her a pallet under one of the wagons. She did not resist and did not complain.

Later, gesturing with her arms and stuttering, Mamshe related how two peasants had caught her and raped her. When she finished telling her story, a look of childish wonder spread across her face, as if she hadn't been talking about herself but about a rumor that she had heard. The women wanted to know more, but Mamshe would add no more to what she had revealed to them. Her face stiffened, and she curled up on the pallet.

"Let her rest," said one of the women, and the others withdrew.

Meanwhile, the old men returned to their low stools and

resumed chanting lamentations. The wagon drivers, who usually don't like to hear lamentations, sat at some distance and listened to the chanting voices. And for a moment it seemed as though they would stop the lamentations and hurry to Mamshe's pallet to beg forgiveness for all the wrongs we had done to her. Now people remembered the Holy Man's admonition: *Look after this young girl, for a precious treasure has been entrusted into our hands and we must deliver her safely to Jerusalem.*

That night was not one of reconciliation. After the old men had returned to their wagons, a loud argument broke out among the dealers. The quarrel was about Mamshe. Some insisted that she be returned to her cage immediately because she was dangerous. Others argued that there was no longer anything to fear from her, that she had changed and should be offered a place in one of the wagons. They spoke of compassion, and of how man is made in the image of God. But the influential ones held firmly to their opinion that Mamshe be returned immediately to her cage. It is impossible, they said, to know what goes on in the mind of a crazy woman.

The following day, the wagon drivers did not slip away from the clearing but fasted, sitting alongside the wagons. They smoked cigarettes and spoke with longing about the distant, forgotten towns where they had been born and from which they had been uprooted years earlier, about their fathers and their fathers' fathers, and about life's twists and turns.

"I don't believe that I'll reach Jerusalem. It looks as if I'll die on the way or drown at sea. The Land of Israel does not admit criminals," said one of the wagon drivers in a voice filled with pain as well as coarseness.

On hearing this, Sruel went over to him and, in a voice that did not seem like his own, rebuked him and said, "What's with you, you fool. We will all reach the Land of Israel. There'll be no exceptions."

"Not me."

"You are a Jew like all the other Jews," said Sruel in a peasant's tone of voice.

"Not me. I've murdered, and there's no forgiveness for murderers, either in this world or in the hereafter."

"Do you think I'm so innocent?" Sruel cried out. "But the Holy Man commanded us to undertake this journey, and we will do as He commanded. Almighty God is great and has compassion for all His creatures." Sruel's eyes blazed with the glow of a man who was fasting.

Then the sun sank down and cast shadows under the wagons. Tzilla sat where she was, mending clothes. There was a quiet in her hands. I was glad that my mother's friend was near me and that I could gaze at the movements of her hands. Suddenly it seemed to me that my mother, too, was standing alongside her and looking at her handiwork, and for a moment I sank into this sweet reverie.

In the midst of this, the mourning drew to a close. The old men returned to their wagons, and all around me people were chopping firewood to set up the bonfires. There was a feeling that the night would be quiet, the dealers would not pursue their dangerous business, the wagon drivers would not quarrel over drink, and the musicians would sit quietly, sipping tea. It seemed to me that without their instruments, the musicians had a defect. During their free time they sit silently, as if all their words have been stripped away.

In the calm of the night after the fast, as people nursed their drinks in their cups and took their first sips of fresh coffee, while everything seemed usual and familiar and without any ominous portent, Mamshe jumped up from her place and fled toward the reeds. Everyone saw her flee but not one person tried to stop her. It was like being in nightmare, with the same feeling of frozenness, of being chained, the same feeling of astonishment that what was happening was beyond our control and who knew what else awaited us.

Though weakened by the fast and casting longing looks at their hot meals, people got up, lit lanterns, and went out to the reeds.

"Mamshe! Where are you?" they called out, waving their lanterns. "Come back to us! We won't put you back in the cage. Don't be afraid!" This time they did not make their way deep into the reeds and did not go along the banks of the river. Their cries hung in the air and slowly grew fainter.

Afterward, people stood silently, as if they expected thunder to pierce the air, but nothing happened. One of the dealers, a man who was sick but very brave, rolled up his trousers and waded into the reeds. Before long, he returned empty-handed.

"She's gone," said someone in a hollow voice, and that was how the search for her ended.

Later that night a woman brought her sick daughter to the old men and asked for a blessing. One of them, a blind one, laid his trembling hands on the girl's head. The girl was frightened and would have run away, but the mother, aware of her fear, held her firmly and would not let go until the old man had finished blessing her.

19

The days passed swiftly. Pleadings and warnings were of no avail, and the old men declared a fast. It was just a few days after the Ninth of Av. The memory of Mamshe's return and her subsequent disappearance still lingered in the air. One of the old men, who had been known as an honest dealer in his youth, took a plank of wood and wrote on it, *Man does not live by bread alone.* He hung it on his body.

Two years earlier, when the old men had declared a fast, detectives and gendarmes had suddenly appeared; they took up positions around the wagons and confiscated goods of considerable value. Since then, people took care not to push the old men beyond their limits. But this time the dealers had been so caught up in their successes, they did not notice the gathering storm. And when they did, it was already too late: detectives and gendarmes pounced on them from every corner.

The struggle between the dealers and the old men, and between the dealers and the gendarmes, had gone on since the convoy first set out. It's true that when the Holy Man was alive, the dealers did not so much as raise their heads; they would pray and study Torah. Although they also traded then, they didn't do it openly, or with such fervor. The Holy Man, who knew them inside out, would rebuke them. But since his death, commerce is all they care about. As the saying goes: *They are enslaved to this passion with heart and soul.* They deal in imported goods, in sugar and spices, in anything at all. They buy and sell from their shabby wagons, and they send out messengers throughout the region. It's true that due to our wanderings and the distances traveled, they would sometimes err in judgment and incur a loss, but it did not discourage them. From year to year they grew more addicted to this drug. You could no longer change them; they were like alcoholics, but it was risk and gambling that flowed in their blood. Now the gendarmes ordered the wagons to be evacuated immediately. Two rounds in the air sufficed to instill fear. In an instant, everyone gathered in the clearing. This time coaxing and bribery were useless. The gendarmes stood their ground: there must be a search.

And it was a thorough one. They knew where to search. They did not touch the old men's and women's belongings, but everything in the possession of the businessmen and dealers was turned inside out. Before long the clearing was piled high with fabrics and clothes, bags of sugar and salt, dried fruit and eiderdown quilts. The gendarmes did not content themselves with this, but carried out body searches as well. Here, too, they did not emerge empty-handed: they cut open coat linings and pulled out gold and jewelry. There was no longer any doubt: the informers had given precise directions to the hiding places.

At noon, the commander arrived to supervise the search in person. Some dealers were arrested and others were beaten. One of the dealers who couldn't take the torture of the interrogation admitted that he had another hiding place not far from the wagons. But even this revelation did not spare him, for the gendarmes had information about still another hiding place, and they went on beating him.

Toward evening three wagons arrived, and with their very own hands the dealers were forced to load the confiscated goods onto them. The pain was intense, but the humiliation was even worse. The dealers, who only the previous day had moved freely from place to place, now stood humiliated and dispossessed.

"It's because of the old men, it's all on account of their wickedness," one of the dealers could not restrain himself from saying.

As always after a robbery, there were the questions: What should we do, and where should we go? The old men stood alongside their wagons as if rebuked; they appeared much older than usual. They prayed in a whisper, and later they shuffled back over to their wagons.

Sruel polished off an entire bottle that night. A clear light illuminated his face, and he served strong coffee and little cakes. People drank and asked for more. It was like after a funeral; there was no fault-finding and blaming, but, instead, a slow submerging into wells of sorrow.

Much later, as a fire burned in Sruel's eyes, he spoke of the holy lights that would shine on us in Jerusalem and of life without gendarmes and without suffering. He spoke simply and in his own voice, but for some reason his words were strained, as if he had rehearsed them. The dealers did not respond and did not argue. They were drowning in their disaster, and his consolations gave them no comfort.

20

The following day, when the dealers awoke from their troubled sleep, they understood that what had happened was not the fault of the old men. Had it not been for some unknown snitches, snakes nestling in our midst, the gendarmes would never have discovered anything. Indeed, some of the dealers in the convoy kept a low profile; they traded in anything, however trifling, and you would always find them, with innocent expressions, where you least expected to see them. In truth, they were spying.

Ever since the convoy had set out, we had been plagued by these men. A year ago, a snitch had been caught on his way to the gendarmes. The wagon drivers followed him, grabbed him, and brought him back to the camp, where he was made to stand before the committee and admit his crime. That night he was beaten up and thrown out of the camp. But all in all, he was just a stinking little fish. A real snitch had yet to be caught. These subversives, or whatever you choose to call them, had wormed their way into our midst. Among them were those who rose early for morning prayers and those who would give alms to the needy; sometimes you'd even find them among those who did volunteer work. But you had to be on your guard: they would eavesdrop on the sly, casually befriending you but all the while piecing together snippets; when the time came, they would snitch. Like thieves, the snitches plied their trade with a multitude of skills; even if you tracked them for months, you'd never be able to follow them. They were as slithery as fish, but their furtive work took its toll on all our lives. Once a year, and sometimes every few months, gendarmes would deploy around our wagons, conduct searches, beat people, and accumulate huge amounts of loot.

And as we did after every disaster, we hitched up the wagons and went on our way in the dead of night. Once again we traveled alongside the Prut. The river was quiet, and the tall reeds along its banks were reflected in the waters. We traveled south. The dismal cloud that had hovered above us since we had arrived in Czernowitz had not dispersed. The quarrels that took place in the wagons were few but fierce. One of the dealers brandished a knife, and another cursed one of the old men with a foul curse.

Eventually, it was decided that the snitch must be found, brought to justice, and taught a lesson; he must be beaten and thrown out of the camp. This would fulfill what was said in our daily prayers, *"And for snitches there shall be no hope."* The lot fell upon a dealer named Ephraim. It was hard to know why. There were several snitches in our midst, but all eyes somehow seemed fixed on him, as if there was no longer any doubt that he alone was capable of something so unspeakable. The dealers and the wagon drivers all felt the same way; even the old men, who were never quick to pass judgment, did not oppose them.

Ephraim did not look like a dealer. He was short and thin, and he appeared younger than his age. Since his childhood he had been haunted by bad dreams, but it was during his adolescence that they completely possessed him and drove him to distraction. Because of his nightmares, Ephraim left the town where he had been born and wandered around the region, scraping by on odd jobs. He did not marry. He reached the Holy Man in Lemberg, who drew him close and told him that he should read a chapter from *The Guiding Lamp* every day. The Holy Man promised Ephraim that reading it would ease his sleep, but that only in Jerusalem would he be completely healed. Meanwhile, the Holy Man advised him not to divulge his distress or misery to anyone. These injunctions, to which Ephraim scrupulously adhered, helped him. Though the nightmares did not cease, his sleep was no longer ravaged. Because of this improvement, his face changed, and an involuntary smile was spread across it. This was something that made him look suspicious from the first month he joined us, and our suspicions only increased as time went on.

Had it not been for the Holy Man's directive, Ephraim would have been cast off long ago, and it would not have been hard to get rid of him. But he was a favorite of the Holy Man, and everyone knew it. When the Holy Man instructed us before his death to look after the children of the poor and take care of them, he was referring to Ephraim, among others. And so despite our suspicions and our aversion to Ephraim's unpleasant expression, no one dared to lay a hand on him.

In time, his smile became a notorious subject of ridicule. Ephraim must have intuited that people were suspicious of him and watching him, for he tried to be pleasant to everyone, to do what was asked of him, and to rise early for prayers. It was strange, but none of this counted in his favor. People invariably said, "He lies awake at night, eavesdropping."

Ephraim traded in dried seeds, nuts, and dried fruit. He would stock up with a few sacks of each kind and sell off his supply in small bags to people in the convoy. During our stopovers, he also sold them to passersby. He always sold at a reasonable price and never tried to overcharge people. His business was not that successful, but he did make a living. From time to time he would give to the needy. The wagon drivers despised him, and the dealers kept their distance, as if from a stranger.

Now it was decided that Ephraim must be interrogated. At first the dealers were of the opinion that he should be handed over to the old men so that they could question him. This was rejected by a majority vote because snitches are extremely cunning and do not own up easily, and in the meantime people might begin to harbor compassion for him. So it was decided to hand him over to two wagon drivers, Shimkeh and Chiyuk, who a while back had been convicted of serious crimes, served time in prison, and had been released after they had completed their sentence.

Shimkeh and Chiyuk consented. Toward evening, they went over to Ephraim and told him that they meant to question him on the matter of the informers, but that before they began their interrogation they would conduct a full search. Ephraim was very taken aback, and with great consternation said, "Absolutely. As you please, you are not strangers. I will show you everything. There is nothing to hide."

"That is for us to judge," said one of them.

They tossed the meager packages out of his wagon and wasted no time in spilling out their contents. But even now, the involuntary smile that always hovered over Ephraim's lips did not leave him. Immediately after that, they searched him. The coins they found were tied up inside a blue handkerchief, and there weren't many.

"May I gather my things together?" asked Ephraim, as though he were a prisoner.

"No" was Shimkeh's answer.

Then the interrogation began. It was conducted under the awning that sheltered the old people during the afternoon hours.

"Why did you snitch?" Shimkeh's opening gambit was devoid of niceties.

"What?" exclaimed Ephraim, a crooked smile on his face.

"If you tell us, we won't beat you."

"I'm a Jew, I would never inform."

"We've seen Jewish snitches."

"I am not an informer."

"Don't smile, tell the truth."

"I swear on my life! You're Jewish, too."

"Tell us the truth and don't swear empty oaths."

"Only apostates inform."

"That's what all snitches say."

All this time, people stayed close to the wagons without uttering a sound. There was the sense that a murky secret was about to burst forth from its hiding place and would soon flood all of us with its darkness. People were afraid of the violent undertone, but were satisfied that so far the wagon drivers had shown restraint and had not beaten Ephraim.

"You say that you didn't snitch," Shimkeh said quietly.

"Correct, absolutely correct."

"But everyone says that you snitched. What do you have to say to this?"

"What can I say?"

"I see that without a thrashing this will go nowhere."

"Don't beat me; I'm weak," said Ephraim, and he moved aside slightly.

"When you snitched you were also weak."

"What can you be thinking?" said Ephraim, catching his breath, immediately surprised that this sentence had come from his mouth.

"We have time," Shimkeh changed his tone. "If you show some remorse and tell us the truth, we won't beat you. What you've done, you've done. If you tell us the truth we'll forgive you."

"What can I say?" said Ephraim, and he covered his

mouth with his right hand. "My father and mother, may their memory be blessed, were God-fearing people. My father wrote *mezuzos* and *tefillin*. He was a poor man but was devoted to his family. He would take me with him to the ritual bath."

"That parents like these could produce such a snitch. . . ."

"I learned the Torah until my bar mitzvah. After my bar mitzvah, I went out to work. I worked as a carpenter, and I helped to support my home. Were it not for the nightmares that tortured me in the dark hours, I would never have left my town. Famous rabbis helped me to sleep a bit, but it was not enough. What could I do?"

"What are you going on about?" He was cut short.

"About my life. Father and Mother were God-fearing Jews; they loved people."

"And you?"

"I am not worth their little finger. I'm dust under their feet."

"So you admit to some of it?"

"They were devoted Jews, heart and soul. I can't compare to them."

"So in that case, why did you snitch?"

"For your information," said Ephraim in a voice that for some reason sounded childish, "I don't have the good qualities of my forebears. They were devoted, heart and soul. But I am not a thief or a gossipmonger."

"I see that without a few lashes there'll be nothing doing this time." Shimkeh changed his tone yet again. "Take off your shirt."

"If you tell me to take off my shirt, I'll take it off. But there's nothing on my body. I'm not hiding anything."

"Take those tales to the old folks. If you don't tell us the truth right away, we'll beat you the way people get beaten in jail—there'd be fifty lashes for snitching."

"Don't beat me," said Ephraim. All at once, his scrawny body seemed to shrink to the size of a child. "Take everything from me. I don't need anything. But don't beat me."

"You don't want to tell us the truth," said Shimkeh as he quickly loosened the belt from his trousers. With no warning whatsoever, he swung it across Ephraim's bare back. The blow must have been strong for it sent Ephraim reeling to the ground. He lay there, shaking. He tried to protect his back with his hands, but to no avail. He began to writhe and to shout.

"Mother! Mother, save me!"

Shimkeh was not satisfied with Ephraim's reaction and gave him a few more lashes, which missed his back but must have hurt his side, because he raised himself in one quick movement, as if the ground had been split beneath him. During the lashes that followed he no longer stirred.

"Get up, you scum!" Chiyuk ordered. He had until now stayed out of the interrogation. Ephraim lay curled up, blood flowing from his exposed back.

"Get up, you scum!" he called again, but Ephraim did not move.

As they emerged from beneath the awning, Shimkeh and Chiyuk were taken aback by the stares they encountered.

"What do you want?" shouted Shimkeh. "That's it. He won't snitch anymore." A wild smile, like that of Ploosh, twisted his lips.

The wagon drivers went on their way, and people hurried to revive Ephraim. Two old men brought a medic, who laid towels on his bleeding back. The towels absorbed the blood and grew red.

"No one should be this cruel to human beings," said the medic. They raised Ephraim's head and rubbed his legs.

"They murdered him," a voice rang out from far off, hollow and grating. The medic got to his feet and the old men stroked Ephraim's arms, which had scarcely been hurt. Someone said to open Ephraim's mouth so that air would get to his lungs.

"We murdered him and we'll pay a heavy price for it," said one of the dealers, who just hours before had been utterly convinced that Ephraim should be handed over to the wagon drivers. Meanwhile, sorrow had given way to fear. People trembled, as if they knew that their days upon the face of the earth were numbered. Even as they stood there stunned, as if waiting for the blow to come down upon them, Ephraim opened his eyes.

"Ephraim!" the old men shouted.

On hearing their voices, Ephraim closed his eyes.

After that, he did not stir from where he lay. The old men took turns watching over him, and the women washed the red-stained towels in the river, dried them on lines, and returned them, white again. Ephraim did not complain and did not cry out. His appearance during the first days after his lashing was like that of a man who had undergone a difficult test and was pleased to have withstood it.

"What should we get you, Ephraim?" people asked him. "Perhaps you'd like to drink?"

Ephraim did not open his eyes. His closed eyes were now stronger than they had been when they were open. The guilt we felt was imprinted on his back, where scabs had formed from the dried blood.

One night, Ephraim burst into little sobs, which shocked the entire camp. The whimpering was like Mamshe's screams when she had tried to break down the door of her cage. The old men tried in vain to calm him. His body trembled. Then Sruel went over to him and said quietly, "Don't be afraid, Ephraim. Soon we'll hitch up the horses and be on our way." It was strange how these words, which were quite beside the point, did the trick. He ceased whimpering.

21

"We must beg Ephraim's forgiveness," said the old men in their quavering voices. The clouds that had hovered over our departure from Czernowitz had not dispersed, and a heavy, dismal rain fell incessantly. The tarpaulins were too narrow to wrap over the wagons, and water seeped into every bundle and every piece of clothing. To our good fortune, we came upon an abandoned sawmill that was empty and spacious and, most important, still had a roof. Many of us, especially the old people, would otherwise have fallen ill.

Ephraim lay at the front of his wagon, his face contorted by pain. People surrounded his bed but for some reason did not dare to ask for forgiveness. Shimkeh and Chiyuk, who had conducted the interrogation, walked sullenly between the wagons but did not apologize.

"We did what we were told to do. It was no more and no less than we were asked. Let no one come complaining to us."

Three days after the lashing, the men from the prayer group gathered alongside Ephraim's wagon.

"Ephraim," my teacher, Old Avraham, said, "we have come on behalf of this sinful community to ask your forgiveness for what we did to you. You do not have to forgive us. We are not worthy of forgiveness, but we would like you to know that our hearts are heavy. We feel tainted, and we wish to mend our ways. We implore you to help us, brother, and God who heals the sick will heal you along with all the Children of Israel who are sick." After my teacher had spoken these words, he withdrew.

Upon hearing all this, Ephraim opened his eyes. It appeared as though he hadn't taken in my teacher's words, or perhaps had not really understood what he said. Everyone waited expectantly for him to say something, but he remained silent. Finally he said, "I'm no longer sick."

"Thanks be to God," said my teacher, without raising his eyes.

The previous year, one of the old men had been abandoned because he hadn't been able to control his bodily functions and had shamed the camp. He was left behind in a small town, in the hope that the Jews there would take pity on him. As it turned out, the Jews did not take pity on him, and he died in the gutter. The bitter tidings caught up with us on the road, and we retraced our steps to bury him. At that time, as well, the old men had surrounded the grave of the man who had died, and they asked for forgiveness. Now it seemed to me that the Ephraim we had known so well had passed away, and this silent, puny man on a pallet, with the look of a sick child, was all that was left of him. What remained was not frightening, because Ephraim himself had never been frightening. A look of wonder had settled onto his face, as if he marveled that his life had turned out as it had. Finally, he came out with a few words that took us all by surprise.

"What happened?" he asked, as if he had awoken from a deep sleep.

"We're here to visit you," said my teacher, happy to have been asked.

"Me?" said Ephraim, and the familiar involuntary smile again creased his face.

"You."

Ephraim closed his eyes, but people still stood there for a long time, remaining quietly beside him.

That night, no one slept. The dealers sought out the old men, wanting to be near them, but the old men had withdrawn into themselves and would not speak. Only Sruel, after a few drinks and in a loud voice, spoke about our future life in the Land of Israel. A different and purified life. And when the falcon landed on his shoulder, he stroked it and spoke to it with great emotion, and promised it a purer life as well. The empathy between them stirred me deeply, and I wept.

I rise early, about an hour before the morning prayers, and record my impressions of our journey in the notebook. Who knows what will turn out to be important and what will prove trivial? Since Czernowitz, my life has changed beyond all recognition. The big city has sunk deep into me, and its dark alleyways leave me feeling unclean.

Now dealers who never used to come to the prayer group have joined. They seek to draw close to the old men. One of the dealers turned to me unexpectedly and said, "Wake me for morning prayers and don't leave me until I get up. Don't let me sleep. Praying is as vital to me as the air I breathe." I glanced at his eyes and I saw that the man spoke the truth.

Once again, I'm at Sruel's beck and call. We work in the fields, plowing and picking plums. Sometimes we bring logs from the groves to the warehouses, always as day laborers. Country Jews are like Ruthenian peasants. They bundle up their money in handkerchiefs, and when they pay Sruel his daily wages, their hands tremble. Sruel asks for more, but they refuse to part with more. In the end, we go our separate ways in peace, wishing them a long life.

When we do not have any work in the fields, I go fishing

with Sruel at the river. One of the old men gave us a present of two small nets and taught us how to spread them. In these parts of the river, the carp are long and narrow, and we sell them cheaply to the people in the convoy.

The evenings are long and filled with twilight, and they spill out over the fields with many hues of purple. Small bonfires give off a scent of dry brushwood, and I pray in my heart that Ephraim's wounds will heal quickly and that he will forgive us. His death and his return to life were very frightening. The old men do not stir from his wagon, as if his existence were a perpetual miracle to be marveled at. For his part, Ephraim blames no one, and does not speak badly of anyone. There is a quiet, deep sorrow in his eyes that flows to us.

In a small village called Halenza, which is near a tributary of the Prut, Ephraim started to utter words the likes of which we had never heard before. He spoke of invisible lights in heaven, lights that nourish the sunflowers and the fruit trees. Were it not for these lights, which are concealed within the revealed lights, we would have neither sunflower seeds nor fruit. Therefore, he said, before every blessing, one should first bless the One who created the light, for without this light there would not be anything over which to say a blessing.

All of us, except for the old men, were astonished. They knew that the agony Ephraim was suffering had transported him to other worlds. In the days that followed, his visions grew even more detailed and more frightening. He spoke of tiny, flickering constellations that descend at night and shower human beings with loving-kindness. Were it not for the light they contain, there would be no healing in the world. These delicate little stars, deer-messengers sent by the angel Gabriel, must be welcomed with affection and gentleness because they intend only to heal. But for anyone who rejected them, and there were people who did so or who were suspicious of them, the living light they bestowed would change to a light of death.

When the old men questioned Ephraim further about these mysteries, he replied simply, "I've seen them." And there was a fearsome certainty in those three words. One morning he told us how he had asked the constellations to give his back more light, and how they had responded favorably and had done so.

Ephraim's pains had almost subsided. But the red welts on his body throbbed and discharged pus and blood. Ephraim blamed himself for not doing enough to appease the constellations that came to heal him during the night. The dealers were ready to take him to Storozhynets, where there was a famous Jewish doctor, but Ephraim refused, saying that it was forbidden to be ungrateful—the constellations would heal him discreetly at night.

Once a day Ephraim would climb down from the wagon. Two dealers would take him to attend to his bodily functions, and he would thank them with little bows. The prayer group came each morning to his wagon. Ephraim had always woken early for morning prayers, but now his prayers took on a different aspect. He prayed without a prayer book, in a whisper and with his eyes open. Everyone stared at him, as if he knew some ancient secrets that had been forgotten. At night they would bring him vegetable soup, a slice of grilled fish, and potatoes. It was hard for him to eat, but to hearten those around him, he made an effort.

22

The convoy made its way slowly and almost aimlessly. In the fields summer crops were being harvested, plums were being picked, and at night the peasants slaughtered pigs with gluttonous joy. Screams and silence could be heard by turns. The broad plain, which had neither towers nor castles, was also full of hiding places, perhaps because of the waterfowl that nested alongside the banks of the Prut and near the marshes.

Only a month earlier the journey had seemed like a chimera, but after the raid by the gendarmes and our own cruelty toward Ephraim, the old men talked openly about Jerusalem. The dealers no longer acted like smart alecks; they were practical men, and our precarious situation worried them. They had changed. This journey would no longer be just another purchasing trip, with its profits and losses. Lurking everywhere were gendarmes and robbers.

Even the nights were no longer as they had been. True, the musicians still played and peasants still gathered around to listen, and we would occasionally receive a few provisions from them. But all the joy was gone. Everything went forward heavily. Even the thieves stole differently. If the truth be told, there was now nothing left to steal. They stole buttons, forks, and spoons, and the following day they would lay everything out not far from where it had been stolen. People no longer bothered to try to find the thieves, or even to reproach them. It was as if our lives were aimless in this regard as well.

We grew poorer, and our food consisted mostly of potatoes and fish from the Prut. Tea was a rarity. We would drink a brew of dried herbs. Sometimes at night a continuous keening that was similar to Mamshe's howls would burst forth from the plain. Everyone knew that sound, but no one spoke about it.

Before we fled Czernowitz, an argument erupted over what to do with the cage. The wagon drivers thought that it should be discarded because it was heavy and useless, but the old men forbade them to do so. One had to admit that without Mamshe the journey was easier; her screams no longer filled our nights with terror. But her absence was felt. The empty cage bore stern witness to her life with us. One of the old men, one of the more silent ones, said with a sigh, "We will no longer have the privilege of seeing her ascend to Jerusalem."

It had not been forgotten that sometimes, on summer afternoons, Mamshe would sit on her pallet and sing. Her angry face would be filled with yearning, and she looked like a woman praying. No one knew her age, who her parents were, and who had brought her to the Holy Man. There were contradictory rumors. As for myself, I can't recall the convoy without her; even now I imagine her curled up on the floor of the cage, dozing.

From time to time, Mamshe would surprise us and ask to be let out.

"Everyone is walking around outside, and only I'm caged in. Why am I the only one caged in?" There were moments when she was not in the grip of her madness, and she would talk and even tell stories. Were it not for her outbursts, she would have been let out, but then people remembered with fear how she had once attacked the two women who took care of her, scratching and biting them. Had it not been for the wagon drivers who rushed to their aid, it is doubtful the women would have emerged without serious injury.

To distract her, people would tell Mamshe, "In Jerusalem you'll be able to walk around to your heart's desire."

"Why?" Her eyes would open wide in wonder.

"Because there everything is holy and everything is good."

On hearing this her mouth would fall open, and her red tongue would dart between her lips.

Even Ploosh's wild laugh was not forgotten. The old men intended to visit him, they even prepared two packages of necessities, but the gendarmes' robbery forced us to flee like criminals. All the same, one of the dealers, by way of his cousin, did manage to smuggle a small package into the prison.

If the truth be told, nothing is ever forgotten here. Our wagons groan beneath the weight of memories; whatever isn't pushed inside has to be dragged along behind us. We remember all those who joined the convoy and abandoned it along the way: the innocents, the crazy ones, to say nothing of those who have slipped quietly out of this world and whom we will see no more.

Now we were all intent on Ephraim's condition. The prayer group gathered around his wagon three times a day. It was a quiet sort of praying, like a prolonged consolation of mourners. Ephraim did not complain, nor did he denounce anyone. He looked like the Ephraim that we knew, apart from his back, of course, where the welts were discolored, swollen, and terrifying.

"How are you, Ephraim?" my teacher, Old Avraham, would ask again and again.

"Thank God."

In a recent dream he had seen soldiers who looked like deserters hiding behind chimneys.

"Were they close by?" asked one of the old men.

"It seemed like it."

"Did they threaten you?"

"I didn't understand what they said to me."

His visions are fearsome, because he speaks of them simply, without exaggeration. Of something that he has not heard or has not seen clearly, he will say, "I didn't hear that" or "I couldn't see." This forthrightness was also a mark of his previous life, but then it seemed like an affectation.

Shimkeh and Chiyuk work for the local landowners during the day, and when they return to the wagons each evening they seem stooped and embittered; they are easily angered and threaten to abandon the convoy if everyone continues to cast blame on them.

"We did what we were told to do," they insist repeatedly. People keep a distance from them, and they spend their nights with the musicians, passing around a bottle and chain-smoking.

23

We straggled alongside the Prut, as if we had lost our way. From time to time the dealers would shake off their reveries and say, "Why don't we travel to Zidova? To Stroznitz? All is not lost." But they were empty words. A hidden despair had burrowed into them. We were at the mercy of the wagon drivers, who were working for the peasants as day laborers and who frittered away their money in the taverns every night. They gave little to charity. "Hurry, *kinderlach*!" the old men would implore them. "Hurry while the rains are still held in the skies." But the wagon drivers paid them no heed; they were arrogant and took no one else into consideration.

Sruel frightened me once, when he asked, "What are you writing, Laish?"

I told him.

"I've forgotten how to write," he confessed. "I forgot everything in prison."

At night, after a few drinks, the wagon drivers would speak of their lives in jail, about the customs and regulations, about the cruelty of the wardens, and about having to obey their slightest whim. There would be no anger in their voices; the years of suffering were buried deep in their large bodies. Now their exterior was just an impermeable blackness from which they would sometimes peek out, as if out of scorched earth, with a wild smile or a groan. Late into the night they stop speaking our language and speak the language of the Ukrainians. I have noticed that when they speak our language, they are terse. They swallow words, get the pronunciation all muddled, and eventually lash out. "The language of the Jews is more like grinding gravel than speaking!"

Truth be told, Sruel belongs with their tribe. When he is in their company he talks like them, uses the words they use, and even gestures as they do. Sometimes it seems to me that he behaves as they do even with the horses. But when he is in the company of the dealers, his expression changes and there's something of his trader forefathers in his eyes. Around the old men, he is bashful; he blushes and purses his lips. Sometimes he asks me about a custom or a law. "Why don't I understand a word of anything the old men teach? I must be stupid." At times he gets angry with himself.

Animals are Sruel's great love. Apart from the falcon that alights on his shoulder every evening and sleeps in his lap, he has two German shepherds who are utterly devoted to him. Any animal that encounters him will nestle against him. Even hornets are fond of him. A few years ago, a swarm of hornets landed on one of the wagons. By a ruse that seemed almost magical, Sruel managed to divert them. In Lemberg he saved us from a pack of stray dogs. He knows how to take care of sick horses, doves, and even snakes. The old men are fond of him, occasionally calling him up to read from the Torah. Were he not addicted to drink, they would be even fonder of him. But what can one say? It seems that he will never be cured of this weakness. As for myself, I have to admit that I love Sruel when he's drunk because, unlike the other wagon drivers, he is very friendly when he's in that condition. When he's cheerful, he likes to make up little ditties. Once I heard Sruel say, "The Jews are my soul's beloved. I'm ready to protect them with all my might. They've suffered so much. Now they deserve a little protection."

The wagon drivers treat him well enough, because despite his strength he will never take anything by force. He has often said to me, "Laish, don't you follow in my footsteps; you must learn from the old men."

Ephraim's wounds haven't healed. I heard him say that it was not the belt that injured him, but the buckle. His very pleasantness scares me. Someone with such deep welts as these should be shouting and not trying to please. I feel my hand tighten into a fist. The old men behave differently. The prayer group gathers alongside Ephraim's wagon three times a day, and after prayers the men drink shot glasses of liquor and then study the Torah.

My teacher, Old Avraham, recently praised me and promised that if I stick with my Torah studies, not only would I be saved from the malicious imps, but my thoughts would be purified and I would be a kosher Jew. If only that were so. But what can I do—my thoughts are still caught up in Czernowitz. The precarious life that the dealers lead still fires my imagination. They have suffered grave losses and now they're melancholy and downcast, and I sense that many will abandon us. *Don't leave us,* I plead in my heart, *you are our only hope. Only you can make a large fortune out of nothing. Only you can fill our pockets with money, bring us to big cities, and help us sprout wings.* They can't abandon us in this wilderness.

The old men can discern even the slightest movement and can sense every restless soul. When they feel that someone is about to abandon us, they climb down from the wagons and stand silently in a circle. Some dealers have already admitted that were it not for the old men, they would have gone back to their towns.

At night on my pallet, I see Maya before my eyes. As always, she is thin, scrawny, with her disheveled hair and her bleak expression. The tumult of feelings she has stirred within me gives me no rest. The feelings are pleasant, to be sure, and they have clung to me from that first evening, when she took off my shirt and called me her cub. These feelings become stronger every time I think of her.

It's now hard for me to see her in my mind apart from the steps on which she sat, or the two green bottles placed next to her, or the frayed collar of her threadbare coat. I see her sitting on the steps, and I'm sorry that she didn't join the convoy. I turn to her. *Maya, why don't you come to us? Our situation may not seem so bright now, but we haven't lost hope. Soon we'll reach a city and everything will change. In the city we become energized. We deal in whatever comes to hand, and our pockets become filled with money. You mustn't worry. We'll welcome you with open arms.* Maya doesn't look at me, and yet I fancy that she's heard what I said. Sometimes I take comfort in the thought that if she does want to join us, it won't be hard for her to find us. People who left years ago have found us. There was a woman named Bronscha who had been left behind at one of our stopovers because she suffered from bad dreams and would curse throughout the night. We didn't hear from her for a whole year. Eventually, on one of our encampments alongside the Prut, she found us. The story she told was chilling. After she had been abandoned, she was raped by a Ukrainian peasant who made her his slave. She lived like this for an entire year. One day, when he noticed that her belly was swollen, he drove her from his house. She spent days wandering about in the marshes near the Prut because her heart told her that she would find us along its banks. And she did find us eventually. When she appeared, no one could believe his eyes: it was Bronscha, and yet it was not her. She told us what had happened to her with a cool matter-of-factness that shocked us all. A month after her arrival she gave birth to a son. On the eighth day he was circumcised and they named him Avraham Yitzhak.

Since the birth of her son, Bronscha's face had become more youthful looking, and she began to prepare hot meals for the old men and the bedridden, who did not have the strength to cook for themselves. The committee has given her a weekly wage. I picture Maya's arrival at our camp like Bronscha's return. Everyone will be surprised—everyone but me. Because I feel that she is already making her way toward us.

24

While the convoy was meandering, going in no particular direction, people began to escape. At this time of year there were always people who escaped. There were also those who would threaten to do so but never carried out their threats. Last year at this time, four dealers, two women, and an old man left. It was as if they had all planned it together. The void that they have left will not easily be filled, and people will always say, *Why did they abandon us?* Of those who have fled, a few returned, but everyone who has been with us is planted in our memory and not forgotten. Occasionally we speak of them as if they were still lying about in their usual places. Sometimes you might hear, *People will soon be starting to escape,* as a kind of warning and alarm. When the threat draws near, the prayers at the evening service become hushed and the men gather in corners, as if, perish the thought, after a funeral. This time the deserters were three dealers and a woman whose pain we knew nothing about. She was a quiet woman who helped the old men and made her living selling trinkets and notions. Her suffering had etched deep lines into her face, but she did not speak of it. Suddenly, without any warning, she joined those who fled.

"What was her name?" someone asked.

"Gusta, don't you remember?"

"I'd forgotten."

In the past, we would have gone after those who had fled and tried to coax them back. Now we have ceased doing this. After we discover who has gone, we sit on the ground and say, *So-and-so has fled* or *So-and-so has also fled*. We sit in a frozen silence. Some years ago, Sruel succeeded in bringing back one of the dealers. For a few days he remained guiltily among us, but in the end he escaped again and no one knows where he is.

The truth must be told: the dealers' situation is now worse than ever. They wander through the villages trying to sell used clothes. When they return in the evening, they look humbled and depressed. Were it not for all the fish that Sruel and I pull from the Prut, we would have nothing to eat. In the evening we grill the fish, and this little happiness puts some light into everyone's eyes.

Our mood is somber, but the troupe plays late into the night. The wagon drivers have taken control of them. They give them food and drink and force them to play. Every night the flutist threatens to flee, but it must be beyond his strength. After midnight he unleashes his wrath on his fellow musicians, cursing his life, Jews, and the convoy.

"Jews have no backbone; instead of working in the fields like everyone else, they wander about in wagons, bringing upon themselves the wrath of all who labor away. No wonder that they are hated, even I hate them. Let them disappear!"

The old men try to calm him down, but their words do little good; they seem only to stoke his anger. Eventually he stands there, shouting, "The Jews are accursed! Their lives are accursed!"

And while the nights were still cold and clear, the plain as flat as after a harvest, wide and without any threatening signs, we were attacked by a gang of robbers. Fortunately for us, the wagon drivers were awake that night and not drunk. They immediately split up: some went to defend the old men and others to do battle. The struggle was short and violent, both sides using daggers. Some wagon drivers were injured and Bronscha and her son were beaten, but there were injuries on the other side, too. Two robbers were left sprawled on the ground, pleading for their lives.

"We'll never so much as touch a Jew again," muttered one of them.

"And who'll vouch for that?" asked Shimkeh in the voice of a dealer.

"We swear on the life of Jesus Christ, our Lord."

"Is this a real oath?"

"May Jesus take revenge on us if we break our oath."

"We'll yet see," said Shimkeh in a chilling voice.

I learned long ago that our wagon drivers are not afraid of death. Their years in prison—the beatings and the backbreaking work—turned them into fearless creatures. The dealers would also sometimes place themselves in danger. I had seen them as they crossed dark forests and crime-ridden neighborhoods; they knew how to give people the slip but not how to fight. Only the wagon drivers would have dared launch into a bloody struggle.

Sometimes it seems to me that the old men are the strongest of us all. Their battle with the Angel of Death is long and courageous, and whenever the Destroyer draws nigh the camp, they gather strength and join together in silent prayer. The way they pray is like a declaration of war. On a few occasions they have abandoned the wagons and turned in the direction of the river to forestall the Destroyer. Although it's true that the Angel of Death is wily and strong, that he sneaks up on the camp to snatch whomever he can, our old men, his main prey, will not go quietly and they do not despair; instead, they stand ready to endanger their own lives to snatch anyone they have the chance of saving from his talons.

But this time it was the wagon drivers' celebration. They were drunk with victory and boasting.

"I grew up among goyim, and I know them well," bragged one of them. "They're no stronger than the Jews." On his own, he recalled other heroic deeds: robbers had once managed to capture two horses and an old woman. After exhaustive searches and some detective work, the dealers went to the captors to negotiate. The bartering went on for days; eventually there was no choice but to give them what they demanded. The woman who had been captured was unhappy with the deal; she argued that her life was not worth a huge amount of money. It would have been better to give the money to those in need and not to waste it on her. In any event, she argued, her days on earth were numbered.

Another time, the Holy Ark with its Torah scrolls was stolen. The old men stood alongside the wagons like soldiers who had failed in their duty, blaming themselves. Beating their breasts, they cried out, "We have sinned! We have committed crimes!" At night the wagon drivers fanned out over the suspected village and grabbed two peasants, who led them to the house where the ark was hidden. When the ark was returned, the old men went forth to greet it with singing, dancing, and drinking. They kept embracing and blessing the wagon drivers, who were as bashful as overgrown children.

Later, they interrogated the wounded robbers, who had, by the way, been bandaged immediately, along with the rest of the injured. It turned out that this gang had been waiting to ambush the convoy ever since it had left Czernowitz, but hadn't dared to attack us because of their fear of the wagon drivers. In the villages, our wagon drivers command respect; they are known as "the strong Jews." This time the robbers had been confident that the wagon drivers had dozed off on their watch, but of course they were mistaken.

Shimkeh turned to the prisoners. "Do you promise never again to do anything bad to the Jews?"

"We swear."

"Who'll vouch for that?"

"God in heaven sees everything and hears everything."

"Remember your oath, and you're free to go," Shimkeh said and freed them from the handcuffs.

Now the wagon drivers swaggered about the camp like landed gentry, baring their muscles, showing off their captured booty, and repeating some well-worn sayings: *A Jew has to be strong and not fearful. Weak Jews bring out the murderer that's in the goy. Strong Jews are good for themselves and good for the goyim.* Their boasts frightened me. Even Sruel, who is not a boaster, was arrogant that evening. He took swigs from his bottle and shouted, "We Jews must be strong; we must eat a lot and drink a lot and give back as good as we get."

25

The convoy veered off the road and then crossed a bridge, delivering itself into the hands of fate. Although this had happened before, this time despair seemed to wash over us. Had we come across a graveyard we would have stopped, prostrated ourselves on the gravestones, and implored the dead to intercede for mercy on our behalf. How strange that only a few days earlier there had been happiness and high spirits, when we had triumphed over the robbers. But immediately after, many sank into gloom and dread. It was as if the light in the sky had been extinguished.

But despair is not a wagon driver's lot in life. After the drivers had routed the robbers, they went to a tavern and got drunk. They returned as completely different people—no longer workingmen but released convicts, singing and carousing, beating our livestock and cursing. The nightly debauchery went on for an entire week, and each day it became more frightening. Attempts by the old men to influence them were in vain.

One evening we saw two peasants approaching us. My teacher, Old Avraham, went over to them.

"Good people, where are we?" he asked.

"What do you mean?" wondered the peasants.

"We've lost our way, good people, and we're looking for the highway."

"You're not far from it, and not far from Vishnitz."

"Thank God," said my teacher, and he blessed them.

Everyone was happy, except for the wagon drivers. Too much religion scares them. In the courtyards of the holy men they are downcast and try to hide themselves. Now they also tried to slip away, but to their chagrin, as the saying goes, the skies opened, unleashing a furious rain, which left them no choice but to urge on the horses.

When the Holy Man of Vishnitz found out that we were on a pilgrimage to Jerusalem, he ordered that we be given shelter and served a hot meal. After days of hunger and being jolted on the roads, the simple refectory where we ate looked like a splendid dining hall. We were starving and devoured everything we were served.

When the Jews heard that a convoy headed for Jerusalem had arrived, they came out of their houses and served us loaves of bread and plum jam. Our herald, Reb Pinchas, was taken aback. It had been a long time since he had appeared in public. He, too, had been sunk in heavy gloom. Now finding his voice, he called out, "Jews, give generously!" And so, once again, we rejoined the ranks of the living. The dealers roused themselves from their reveries and asked about the price of sugar and salt. The old men gathered around Ephraim's pallet and prayed aloud. Only the wagon drivers were dejected. Bundled up in their coats, they sat at the back of the wagons, taking swig after swig from their bottles.

That night, the Holy Man of Vishnitz spoke to us. He talked about darkness, and about the smothering materialism that keeps the light from us and turns us into slaves of body, property, and money. Our daily lives, he said, are like those led by the slaves in Egypt. But anyone who is able to summon up the courage to leave his town and go on a pilgrimage to the

Land of Israel restores to the world the light from the Exodus from Egypt. And if those who were drowning in darkness and impurity could only smell the Red Sea, they would be invigorated and elevated to a meaningful life.

There was silence after the Holy Man had finished speaking. Sruel grasped my forearm.

"What did the Holy Man say?" he asked.

I didn't know how to reply. I had understood the Holy Man's words; I just didn't know how to explain them. But I gave it a try. Sruel slapped his forehead.

"Why can't I understand a word of what he said?" he asked. "I must be stupid."

Later, the dealers asked Reb Pinchas to enact the biblical story of Joseph. Pinchas excused himself, saying, "I'm very tired and my mouth is empty of words."

Entreaties were useless. But the musicians, who had been temporarily freed from the tyranny of the wagon drivers, lost no time. There was a mournful sweetness to the way they played that brought tears to people's eyes. Even the old men, who rarely allowed themselves to open their hearts, wiped away tears.

We felt a sense of relief, as if we had returned home. On the following day people pampered us as well, gazing at us with excitement and astonishment. My teacher, Old Avraham, did not conceal from those who stared at us with such wonder that the road was full of potholes, and that heaven only knew what trials awaited us. He didn't speak about what had happened to Ephraim; he just repeated that there had been many hindrances and delays, both from within and without, but that with the help of God, we would be delivered.

The wagon drivers gave their horses water and did not intervene in what was going on. They took swigs from their bottles and fell asleep wherever they happened to be. The musicians played on until late; their playing was slow and reflective. Each with his own instrument told of their hardships from the outset of the journey—about the humiliations and degradations, and about the wagon drivers who forced them to play with the very last ounce of their strength.

Ephraim's back had not healed; the blue welts had returned, and they were swollen. He kept speaking about his father and mother and the little town where he had been born, and about the nightmares he had suffered in his childhood and as a youth, which had driven him to flee from his home and wander from place to place. There was neither confusion nor anger in his words, but it sounded like a story with a bitter moral. The prayer group listened with a frightening silence to the words that welled up from inside him.

That very night one of the dealers made his escape. Pinyah was his name. A confirmed thief, he had a particular weakness for buttons. He could pull them off with great skill and without tearing the garment. No one escaped his forays. He was not an arrogant man, and he dealt in household goods. He seemed honest enough. He would give generously to charity, and sometimes he would prepare a meal for the sick, but he was unable to overcome his weakness. On more than one occasion it was decided to banish him from the convoy, and once he was even beaten by one of the wagon drivers, who threw him and his belongings off the wagon. But in the end he was not sent away. Everyone knew that only he stole buttons, but people could not bring themselves to confront him. A rumor circulated that he had a bag full of buttons; according to another version, he didn't keep the buttons but buried them in the ground. There were many thieves among us, even an elderly thief, but we had only one button thief, and for some reason he ran away.

26

We were not in a hurry to leave Vishnitz. The musicians played late into the night and the local people brought us all kinds of good things. The dealers, who for days on end had been plunged into the deepest gloom, once again began to circulate, buying and selling, and at night stuffed their coins and bank-notes into the pockets of the old men. For most of the day, the old men sat in the synagogue, studying Torah and dozing.

In the morning, after prayers, I set out with Sruel to fish in the Prut. These quiet hours open my eyes, as Sruel tells me of his life in jail. His eyes are blue and affectionate, and he doesn't speak pridefully. The sun and the waters of the Prut have beaten his face and neck to a coppery texture. He's strong, and his strength is evident in all his movements. When we brought the fish to the clearing, he announced, "Fresh fish! Straight from the Prut!" The air was filled with his voice.

The following day he bought me a pair of shoes and two shirts. I wanted to thank him but I didn't know how. Finally I said awkwardly, "Thank you very much, Sruel."

"You should be studying Torah," he said, as if rebuking me.

"I do study."

"You have so much to learn."

. . .

My teacher, old Avraham, now spends most of his day performing ritual immersions and studying. I dare not approach him. Since we arrived in Vishnitz he has devoted himself completely to the Torah. I gaze at him from afar and my head starts to spin.

"Laishu, my son, where are you?" he called to me.

"I'm here."

"Be so good as to bring me a glass of water."

When I brought him the cup, he closed his eyes and made a blessing over the water, and I saw with my own eyes how the radiance of the Torah glowed on his forehead.

While the evening light grew red in the sky and as people began preparing their meals, a man who bore a great resemblance to Ploosh emerged from the thicket. But his appearance was a bit different. A heavy beard adorned his face, and the beard and the fur hat made him look like a peasant who had come to survey his distant fields. There was not the slightest bit of animation or anxiety in his eyes.

One of the wagon drivers approached him carefully. "What happened, Ploosh?"

"I ran away," said Ploosh, and a wild smile spread across his hairy face.

"And where are you now?"

"No place," he said, his smile becoming even wilder.

This reply momentarily silenced the inquisitive wagon driver, and he looked around, seeking the help of his friends who stood near him. Everyone was seized with a feeling of amazement.

"What happened?" asked Ploosh, as if focusing on some irregularity.

"Nothing. How did you find us?"

"I know these parts like I know the back of my hand," he said in a peasant's tone of voice.

"And what do you want to do?" asked the wagon driver in the same tone of voice.

"Nothing."

All his words used up, a profound silence surrounded him. Ploosh knew the people who had gathered around him very well. With some he had worked, drunk, and played cards; the others he had driven in his wagon. True, no one was fond of him, but since his imprisonment, people's attitudes toward him had softened. They spoke of him as a wild man who didn't know how to control his emotions. And while everyone was still in the grip of their amazement, Ploosh fixed his gaze on me and said, "What are you doing here, Laish?"

I froze where I stood, but I must have stumbled, because some men picked me up and shouted, "What do you want from him?"

"Nothing," said Ploosh, and his smile softened a little. "Are you afraid of me?" he added.

Then he sat with the wagon drivers and told them about his adventures, beginning with the day that he escaped from the jail. The wagon drivers plied him with questions, and Ploosh gave them all the details. At first he had worked in the prison yard and had gained the trust of the man in charge of it. The next stop had been the kitchen. The doors to the kitchen were open most of the day and were close to the rear gate of the jail. Provisions and furniture would be brought in through the rear gate, and here the guards were less careful.

Ploosh's escape had been as simple as could be. One night there was a delivery of beds and pallets to the storeroom. At first, the guard refused to open the gate. The peasant, an old man, would not yield. He claimed that he'd wasted an entire day coming from the main warehouse. Had they told him that they wouldn't open the gate at night, he would never have come. The argument lasted a long time. Eventually the guard took pity on the old man and opened the gate. The kitchen door was open and no one but Ploosh was there. While the peasant was arranging the furniture in the storeroom, Ploosh jumped onto the wagon and made his escape. The horses took fright and galloped as if crazed, until they sank into the marshes.

On hearing the story of Ploosh's escape, the faces of the other wagon drivers became flushed with happiness, and they looked as though they were about to cheer him. Ploosh gestured dismissively with his right hand, as if to say, *That's just how it is. It's not like it was something that a very clever man might have done. You do it because you do it. You don't fool yourself into believing that you acted with great wisdom.*

I knew this gesture of his all too well, but now it came with additional force, as if it had been honed. Then the talk turned to wise and foolish people—wise people whose wisdom had led them astray and foolish people whose foolishness had saved them. Ploosh seemed to grow in stature that night. While he was gone, his forehead had broadened and his gaze had sharpened; he was like a peasant upon whom many misfortunes had fallen, but they had not managed to break his spirit.

Prior to this evening, Ploosh's standing among the wagon drivers had not been particularly lofty. Now they stared at him, marveling at what came out of his mouth, asking questions, and listening without interrupting. Ploosh spoke at length, but without going into too many details. His trial was in its first stages. The prosecutor never hid the fact that he intended to demand the death penalty. When one of the wagon drivers asked if he was afraid, Ploosh replied unhesitatingly, "I'm not afraid. Fear is loathsome."

That night they drank freely, laughed, and reminisced about days past. And of course about jail, the wardens, the junior wardens, the snitches, and the punishments. Ploosh drank moderately and kept his wits about him. He asked for neither help nor shelter. He knew that a man does not return to the place from which he was taken away in handcuffs to ask for refuge. The wagon drivers entertained him but expected that after the meal he would take himself off. And so he did.

Ploosh rose to his feet. "Must be going," he said.

The wagon drivers also rose to their feet. One of them took a wad of banknotes from the lining of his coat and tried to give some of them to Ploosh. Ploosh narrowed his eyes, glared at the wagon driver, and said, "We don't need any charity. Worry about yourself first; I will overtake my prey."

Without further ado, as if merely going off to a day's work, Ploosh plunged straight back into the thicket. Without saying a word, the wagon drivers followed him with their eyes as he disappeared.

27

The following day I again went to the Prut with Sruel. He was withdrawn and sullen. I knew of Ploosh's enmity toward him, but I didn't see any sign that portended ill. I helped Sruel spread the nets, and at ten o'clock I prepared break-fast. Even during his meal the sullenness did not lift from his face.

When he had finished the meal, Sruel's lips suddenly pursed into a smile of sorts, and he said, "Ploosh hates me. I don't know why he hates me. I've done him no harm." After a short pause, he added, "He has hated me all these years. Mur-derers hate human beings."

Yesterday he didn't hate you, I was about to say, but I bit my lip. I've already learned: eyes can be shortsighted. A carefully nurtured animosity can seethe for years. And then suddenly, and for no apparent reason, it can burst forth like a storm. Even our herald, Pinchas, a pleasant man who is well liked by the occupants of all the wagons, even he harbors a grudge against one of the quiet, miserable dealers. One day he went over and slapped the wretched man's face.

I would soon learn the extent to which Sruel was right. That afternoon, near the wagons, a man's voice suddenly rent the silence. Immediately thereafter we saw Ploosh, standing in plain view on the opposite bank. He looked like an escaped prisoner, perhaps because of the fur cap on his head.

"What do you want?" called Sruel in a firm voice.

The answer came without delay.

"Scum!"

That solitary word, spat out by Ploosh in his strong voice, rang out clear. But Sruel must have been so surprised that he could not comprehend it.

"What do you want?" Sruel called again.

Again, the answer was not long in coming.

"Are you still asking, you scum?"

Now, too, Sruel seemed not to understand the curse and asked yet again, "What do you want?"

"The reckoning will come, you scum! We'll meet again."

Now, finally, Sruel understood and, rallying quickly, he replied, "Son of a whore!"

"Thief!" Ploosh shouted.

"Murderer!" Sruel flared back at him.

"Horse thief!"

"Murderer of women!"

"Thieving son of a thief!"

The exchange of curses went on and on. Eventually Ploosh fell silent and slipped away into the thicket. Sruel's face was red and his hands shook. He collected the nets and then picked them up with one motion. I knew that "horse thief" was the foulest curse that there was and that peasants don't use it unless they're at the end of their tether.

When we returned to the wagons, Sruel gave the fish away to anyone who asked. He gave with an open heart. He didn't regard the fish as plunder for which he had labored for many hours, but as if they were supplies that belonged to the entire camp. The darkness had lifted from his brow, but his mouth remained shut. When people offered to pay him, he made a gesture of refusal that seemed akin to a rebuke.

After Sruel distributed the fish, I prepared a cup of coffee for him. He thanked me, but didn't invite me to sit at his side. When I returned after about an hour, he was already fast asleep beneath a tree. He lay curled up, his height and his powerful build barely noticeable.

That night was clear and lofty, and the Holy Man of Vishnitz came out into his courtyard and spoke to us about the highest places in the world. He spoke of God, blessed be He, who can be found everywhere, even in clods of earth or the crevices of a rock, and about how there is not the slightest tremor in the world that He does not cause. It is therefore good, he said, to commit one's body and soul to God each day from early in the morning, and to neither worry nor be afraid. Worry and fear are wretched feelings that cloud one's vision and hearing. Without clear-sightedness and lucid attentiveness, we would be unable to take in the marvels that are constantly occurring around us and to hear the sacred melodies that rustle through the crops and the saplings.

After the Holy Man finished speaking, there was silence. No one stirred. Sruel grabbed my arm.

"Did you understand what he said?" he asked.

"A little," I replied, for my teacher had taught me to listen.

"What did he talk about?"

"About God, blessed be He."

"I was told that it's forbidden to pronounce His name."

I did not know what to answer and I said, "The Holy Man also spoke about worry and fear."

"I'm not afraid," said Sruel in a wagon driver's tone of voice, and he turned away.

But I was afraid that night. The Holy Man's words could not remove Ploosh's fearsome appearance from my head. It seemed to me that he was crouching in the thicket alongside the wagons and was about to storm them, to send them flying, and then to crush them. In my memory of him standing bare-chested on the banks of the Prut, he looked like a giant.

That night Sruel drank a lot, but it didn't lift his spirits. He cursed Ploosh and swore that if he ever ran into him, he wouldn't take pity on him, because he was an abhorrent murderer, and it was only right to turn murderers over to the gendarmes. His drunkenness scared me.

We were summoned in the middle of the night by one of the old men, who stood in the clearing and cried like a child. His money, which had been sewed into his coat, had been stolen.

"I didn't have much and now I have nothing," he wailed.

Sruel tried to calm him down. "We'll help you out."

But the old man would not be consoled.

"Until now I was never in need of charity," he muttered in a shattered voice. "But from now I will be forced to hold out my hand."

"Don't be afraid." Sruel spoke to him in a voice that was different from his own.

"Why did he steal from me?" He could not stop whimpering.

Sruel drew a banknote from his trouser pocket and thrust it into the old man's hand.

The old man was dumbstruck by this, and said, "That's not my money. That's not the money that I saved up."

"It can stay with you until the thief returns what he stole."

"The thief won't give it back to me. They never give things back."

The next day the old man rallied and wanted to return the banknote to Sruel. Sruel refused.

The old man grabbed Sruel's arm and said, "You gave me more than was stolen from me."

"An extra penny won't hurt you."

"I'm afraid to keep so much money on me."

"I'll look after you. I'll cut off the fingers of whoever dares to steal from you."

"Heaven forbid!"

"There will be no redemption for the wicked."

"But not by force, not sheer force, my dear friend."

"Then how?"

"Calmly and quietly."

"So be it," said Sruel, and we immediately went back to the tasks that awaited us.

28

Ephraim's wounds did not heal. They brought in a village medic, and the man rubbed a yellow ointment on his back. Some of the old men were of the opinion that we should seek the Holy Man's advice, but people were afraid. If Ephraim wants to ask, let him ask; we don't have to ask for him. Ephraim's wounds were changing color; they were yellow now.

Meanwhile, Ephraim was no longer lost in his visions. He would doze for most of the day, curled up on his pallet. During prayers, he would raise the upper part of his body and pray with his eyes closed.

"How do you feel?" my teacher, Old Avraham, would ask him from time to time.

"Good," he would answer, and open his eyes.

Ephraim's sleep was somehow scarier than his visions. Before he sank into slumber, he would speak of the pus that must be drained from an infected body and of the purified blood that washes the arteries clean. The awe of youth radiated from his eyes, as if all his years had been stripped away from him. Later, when Ephraim fell asleep, Blind Menachem stayed constantly by his pallet. Ever since Ephraim's visions had started, Menachem had been tense, attentive to every word that came out of Ephraim's mouth. Now that his visions had subsided, Menachem was filled with anxiety.

"How is Ephraim doing?" he would ask. "What is he saying?"

At Sruel's bidding, I would bring them grilled fish and potatoes every evening. After the meal, Menachem would be taken to the clearing, where the story of Joseph's sale into slavery was again being presented.

Pinchas had revived the play and changed it completely. He enlisted several wagon drivers and two dealers. Dressed in shabby fur coats, they become the sons of Jacob. They stand alongside the pit and look like a violent gang tracking its prey.

Blind Menachem continues to play our forefather Jacob. He sits on a chair, a footstool supporting his feet, looking like an abandoned father whose sons have grown up wild.

People gather around, both Jews and non-Jews. Once again, the audience is spellbound by the performance. Two wagon drivers have put up a gate, and they charge an entrance fee. Late at night they divide up the earnings among the director, the actors, and the guards. Naturally, there are differences of opinion on the division of the proceeds, but eventually a compromise is reached and everyone returns to his wagon.

Sometimes the audience lingers after the performance, crowding in on the actors, asking them questions and complimenting them, and putting money in the charity box. It's hard for those who dwell in houses to understand how a man can leave his home, his plot of land, and sally forth into the unknown. Sruel's answer is simple and straightforward.

"A Jew must return to Jerusalem. But what does he do? He sits and waits for the Messiah to come. It's true, the dangers are great, and villains and wicked people lurk in every corner, but a Jew has to overcome his fears and do as he has been instructed."

I have noticed that whenever Sruel is feeling heady and

enthusiastic, he uses the few words that he has acquired from the old men. The other wagon drivers don't like to be asked questions; they either shrug people off with a dismissive gesture or they say, "Ask the old men and don't ask us wagon drivers."

Just as the actors were dispersing, the wagon drivers preparing for their night's revels, and the musicians tuning their instruments, Ploosh leaped out of the thicket. He headed straight for our wagon, and when he saw that the horses were not there, he cried out, "Where are my horses?"

Fortunately for us, the wagon drivers had not yet begun drinking, and when his frightening voice was heard they were quickly summoned and they came. Seeing all the people who had gathered around him, Ploosh drew a revolver from his belt.

"Give me my horses right now!" he said threateningly. Ploosh the murderer was back. Fire blazed in his eyes, and he stood there as tense as a predator about to spring.

"Which horses do you want?" Shimkeh ventured to ask.

"Mine."

"We'll give them to you right away."

"And where's that scum?"

"Who?"

"Sruel."

"He's here. Should we get him?"

"Don't move."

"We won't move."

"I also need money."

"How much?"

"Everything."

"The dealers will give you some. Don't worry; they have. Should we wake them?"

"Stand where you are and don't move, you thieves!" Ploosh shouted in his powerful voice.

"The dealers have a lot of money. As much as you want," Shimkeh said in a friendly way.

These words slightly relaxed Ploosh, and he spat out a curse. Chiyuk took advantage of this momentary lapse of attention to leap on him. Though Ploosh managed to pull the trigger and fire a shot, Chiyuk was tougher and held on until he had strangled him.

Fortunately for us, it was a dark and rainy night; the shot was muffled and not heard by the gendarmes. The wagon drivers remained standing for a long time beside the outstretched corpse. Ploosh lay sprawled on the ground, his mouth open, his eyes wide open. Only his motionless limbs bore witness to the fact that he was dead. What's to be done? The question sliced into the void. Chiyuk, who had carried out the strangulation, did not participate in the conversation. He stood to one side, as if expecting someone to approach him. But everyone was preoccupied with what to do with the body and no one paid any attention to him.

It was eventually decided to bury Ploosh in the forest. The gendarmes were always looking for things to accuse us of and for ways to extort money from us. But the old men were completely opposed to this. Even when he sins, a Jew remains a Jew, and we should give him a Jewish burial. The wagon drivers were far from happy, but they were afraid of disobeying. Early in the morning Ploosh's body was ritually washed, and he was given a Jewish burial in an old, neglected graveyard.

After the burial, a heavy rain fell and the entire convoy set to work fastening the tarpaulins over the wagons. Everyone worked rapidly, but the rain got into everything and soaked both provisions and clothes, and there was a strong feeling that Ploosh would not leave us alone, not even in death.

That same rainy day, many Jews came to ask the advice of the Holy Man of Vishnitz: a typhoid epidemic had broken out in the region and everyone was gripped by panic. It was as if we had been forgotten. People swarmed around the Holy Man's doorway like bees.

"We had best clear out immediately," was the opinion of many.

The old men admonished them. "We must wait for the blessing of the Holy Man."

Meanwhile, we tried to dry out the clothes and to salvage our provisions from the dampness. The wagon drivers were happy that Ploosh's death had passed unnoticed and that the Holy Man had been preoccupied with other matters.

"We've been saved from the hands of the gendarmes!" someone said in a coarse voice.

After days of waiting and hoping, the old men agreed that there was no chance of an audience with the Holy Man and that we had best slip away. We hitched up the horses and fled like thieves. Sruel, who had been tense the entire time, suddenly said in a strange voice, "He hated me. Why did he hate me?"

"He must have thought that you wouldn't give him back his job."

"What nonsense! It was his, not mine."

"So he was wrong. That's all."

29

Once again we make our way along the Prut. Sruel urges the horses on, brandishing his whip on them. The sated horses amble along the dusty road, and the reeds recede into the distance. The strange death of Ploosh weighs on us and gives us no rest. We live in fear of the gendarmes, of robbers, and of the strangled Ploosh. Sometimes it seems to us that he has not been strangled but has retreated to the thicket to regain his strength, and that the day will come when he'll emerge with one of his friends, a fellow convict from jail, and take his revenge on us.

I see the anxiety in Sruel's eyes. He goes about justifying himself, as if it were he and not Chiyuk who had strangled Ploosh. Chiyuk wastes no time on regrets.

"If I hadn't killed him, he would have killed many others. If someone comes to kill you, rise early to kill him," he asserts unpleasantly. He has hung Ploosh's revolver from his belt. I've already heard him boasting, promising that from now on he'll defend the camp and that there is nothing to fear.

My teacher, Old Avraham, says that Ploosh did have some sparks of righteousness, but that the murderer in him extinguished them. I recall that sometimes Old Avraham would sit and talk with Ploosh. He was among the few who became close to him. Other old men tried but gave up. From the depths of despair, they said something that they rarely say: *Not even Jerusalem will cure him.*

I'm afraid of Chiyuk. He now seems like a reincarnation of Ploosh. He is not tall either, though he is stocky and swaggers around the camp like a tyrant. Since he strangled Ploosh, people keep their distance from him. For his part Chiyuk seeks out the old men, and, whenever he has the chance, he thrusts coins into their hands.

Sleep has given Ephraim more strength. Now he speaks of the typhoid epidemic that threatens us, admonishing us to keep away from the villages and the small towns. There is a chilling certainty in his voice. But we do keep our distance from the smaller settlements and we buy only the most vital provisions: potatoes and cornmeal. In these parts of the river, fish are not plentiful; people are quick to buy them, and they grill them right away.

Without our being aware of it, the High Holy Days have come upon us. The old men have taken their white clothes out of their bundles and washed them in tin pails. During these days a severity burns in their eyes. They spend less time studying and more time visiting the sick, helping the needy, and trying to coax the wagon drivers into forgiving their companions because it is indeed forbidden to harbor enmity, particularly at this time of year. They urge the dealers to give charity and to imagine that their dead forefathers—God-fearing Jews who kept both the easy and the most stringent commandments— are standing before them. There was a time when the dealers would argue with them, but now they nod with gloomy indifference. The old men live off their savings and worry about the future, yet they still give. One good word to them from the wagon drivers would have rejuvenated them. But the wagon drivers are too preoccupied with their own affairs, and whenever they encounter a peasant along the way, their first question is always "Where's the tavern?"

Meanwhile, the rain falls incessantly, and there is no shelter. This is a region of plains, without trees and without abandoned houses—only thickets and marshes—and the waters of the Prut wend their way to the sea. The tarpaulins, which are the pride of the wagon drivers, provide no cover, even when their sides are pulled tight. The smallest tear can soak you to the skin. But not to worry. When the rains cease and the sun comes out, we stop the wagons and hang the wet clothes on ropes that have been stretched out, grateful for the respite from the rain.

"Give to the needy, give to the sick," the old men plead over and over. Not that there's always someone to heed their voices.

These days, anxiety dwells within Sruel's eyes. He helps fill the pails with water, chops wood, and distributes our fish for free. The old men shower him with blessings. They don't rebuke him now, even when he has had a drink too many.

Last night, the wagon drivers offered me some vodka and Sruel scolded them.

"It won't hurt him," said one of the wagon drivers.

"He needs to study Torah. Vodka dulls you."

"A man needs a drink at night. Without a drink you're a limp rag," muttered the wagon driver.

"You should know better—a Jew doesn't drink." Sruel spoke in an authoritative voice.

"I'm no longer a Jew." The wagon driver made an odd grimace.

"We may be Jews who've gone bad, but we're still Jews." Sruel chose to speak in the plural.

Two days before Rosh Hashanah they halted the wagons, and we made camp in a narrow enclave by the water. I watched

Bronscha's child, Avraham Yitzhak, who had been born after the rape, running around between the wagons. He must have been about three at the time, his face sunburned, his small body firm and sturdy. Every evening Bronscha would bathe Avraham Yitzhak and then bring him to the old men. The old men would envelop him in a prayer shawl and show him the large letters in the prayer book. The child would wriggle in their arms and try to get away. Eventually he would break free. Bronscha would run after him, catch him, and give him a slap on the face.

"Don't run away, you little criminal! You should be studying Torah and not running around between the wagons."

At first Avraham Yitzhak would try to restrain himself, but eventually he would burst into tears.

"What's to be done?" asked Bronscha in despair. "He's completely wild."

"Go slowly." The old men tried to persuade her.

Around the old men, Bronscha did not beat Avraham Yitzhak. But late at night, alongside her wagon, she did not hold back. She would take all her anger out on him, slapping his face and pinching his bottom and threatening to knead his flesh until he behaved. There were two other children Avraham Yitzhak's age in the convoy, but they were shorter and weaker than he, and whenever Avraham Yitzhak would appear, they would run to their mothers screaming in terror.

Bronscha worked for the old men for most of the day. She cooked for them and did their laundry, and quarreled with the convoy's committee for being stingy and not giving her the provisions she needed. But she got along well enough with those on her wagon. Whenever she had some leftover soup or vegetable pie, she would give it away willingly, but if people complained that her Avraham Yitzhak had been beating up the other children, she would go crazy. Her face would become pale, her hands would tremble, and she would pounce on him with unrestrained fury. She would not stop until her wagon mates intervened.

"Let him be, Bronscha," they would plead. "Enough already!"

30

Before Rosh Hashanah, Bronscha was busy ironing the old men's white linen. The wagon drivers had prepared an ironing table for her well in advance, and they spread a heavy blanket on it. Bronscha would rise early, along with those who prayed, and stand by the table until dark. The smell of coal and starch wafted throughout the camp, bringing to mind Rosh Hashanahs from long ago. Quite a few people have passed away over the years, and quite a few abandoned the convoy. I remembered my first employer, Fingerhut, who left this world seething with anger, and I felt my heart tighten. The memory of him is all but gone, but occasionally you will hear, *Give charity! Don't be wicked like Fingerhut!*

People never called Fingerhut by his first name, not even those who accorded him a little kindness. Here, at least, people do not think fondly of him. Over time he turned into an example and a warning. But I felt sorry for him because he was in such pain. The old men slip out of this world differently, furtively, like the morning mist. When one of them is recalled, people say, *May his memory be for a blessing,* and his image immediately appears before you and you know that there is purity in the world.

. . .

The Days of Awe were upon us. Everyone gathered around the old men, and they seemed to grow in stature until they resembled the ancient priests as they rose to bless the nation. But things were not now as they once were. We were haunted by the murder of Ploosh. People didn't speak of it, but there was a feeling that the typhoid epidemic was being carried on the wings of Ploosh's furious spirit and that it was about to attack us. This terror has been mounting from day to day. Ephraim's visions reveal it clearly, with explicit descriptions. And it's not only him: a few of the dealers have complained of nightmares. Who knows who will live and who will die? Who knows if in a month's time we will be walking in the land of the living?

The Prut is already chilly at this time of year but people bathe in it every day. They believe that its waters will purify their body and drive away the plague. It's a belief that has gained much ground in the past few days, but of course there are those of little faith who stand to the side and don't trouble to go down to immerse themselves. They prefer a large pail. "Better a little warm water in a pail than waves of ice water," they say as they take cover in the thicket.

The old men ritually immerse themselves in the river as usual, once a day, without talking much about it. They are absorbed in their preparations for the holiday. They whisper their prayers, visit the sick, and ask forgiveness of all who cross their path. There is nervousness in their every step; it's as if they are standing before the gates of judgment, which are about to open with a great clamor.

Ephraim is very embarrassed. Everyone comes to ask for his forgiveness.

"I forgive you with all my heart," he says, "but you also have to forgive me."

There's not a trace of anger in his voice. Shimkeh and Chiyuk haven't gone over to him. The old men have not stopped begging them to do so, but they keep refusing.

"We have nothing to say to him," said Chiyuk.

"You owe this to yourselves."

"Let everyone else ask first."

"They've already asked."

"We didn't notice."

In the end they gave in to the old men's entreaties.

"What should we say to him?" asked Chiyuk, who had been a party to the interrogation although he had not taken part in the beating.

"Just say, *We ask your forgiveness, Ephraim.*"

"That's all?"

"That's all."

"And if he asks us something, what should we reply?"

"Ephraim doesn't ask. You have nothing to fear."

In the afternoon Shimkeh and Chiyuk sat under a tree and took swigs from a blue bottle of vodka. Huddled in their coats, they looked heavy and unkempt. I felt sorry for them. Whenever there's a need for brute force, people call on them. On several occasions they have saved the convoy from highway robbers, but they were never truly welcome. Never was their heroism praised in the way that people rejoice in the success of the dealers. Not that the dealers are as pure as the threads of prayer shawls, but it's easy to forgive them. Now Chiyuk has to bear the weight of a fresh accusation: Ploosh. People keep their distance from murderers, even when they have murdered for a good cause, even if they have saved many lives. Once I heard Shimkeh say, "We have to take a double thrashing: once in this world and once in the world to come. Never mind, we've been given strong bodies. They can take it."

Toward evening Shimkeh and Chiyuk approached my teacher, Old Avraham. "We're ready."

"I'll come with you."

My teacher began by saying, "Shimkeh and Chiyuk have come to ask your forgiveness, Ephraim."

"Why?" said Ephraim, the familiar involuntary smile playing about his lips.

"That's what they have to do. Speak, Chiyuk, speak," my teacher prompted him.

Chiyuk lowered his head and stood stock-still.

"Tell Ephraim what you wanted to say. Don't be embarrassed."

"I'm not embarrassed," said Chiyuk, and he raised his head.

"So say it."

"Say what?" said Chiyuk, as if he had forgotten what they had agreed on.

"Tell him that you ask for his forgiveness."

"All right."

The old men who stood alongside them lowered their heads, as if they expected a clap of thunder to set the place to shaking. And the shaking-up was not long in coming.

"If everyone will ask forgiveness, then we will, too," said Chiyuk in a loud voice.

"Everyone has already asked." He was hurriedly cut short by one of the old men.

"It's not fair, but I'm willing. I don't care."

Shimkeh, who until that moment had not uttered a word, said, "We aren't guilty. We did what we were told to do. Those who were beaten should know this."

"He knows, he knows everything," my teacher said impatiently.

"If that's so, then why does he need our forgiveness?" replied Chiyuk.

"*He* doesn't need anything," said my teacher with restrained anger. "*You* need it."

"We're lost causes, anyway," said Chiyuk, making a gesture of dismissal with his hand. Hearing the certainty in Chiyuk's voice, Ephraim propped himself up on his right elbow and said, "Thank God, we have enough to eat and a pallet to sleep on. We lack for nothing, and soon we'll be able to buy some nuts and seeds, and go back to trading like before."

Chiyuk, who could not have understood Ephraim's words, said, "What do you want from us? We only did what they told us to do to you. You should blame everybody else, and not just us."

"Enough," said my teacher, trying to hush him.

"We sinned, but it wasn't just us."

It seemed as though Ephraim wanted to say something else, but when he saw that the crowd was dispersing, he again lay down on his right side, a movement that immediately exposed the injuries on his back.

31

On the eve of Rosh Hashanah, the wagon drivers prepared a table for the Torah, a lectern, and benches to sit on. We quickly set up the tent, and the clearing that had been open to the four winds unexpectedly shrank, bringing to the mind rainy Sabbaths and holy days. Sullen, Shimkeh and Chiyuk kept close to their wagons, taking no part in the work at hand. Ever since they stood face-to-face with Ephraim, the somberness had not lifted from their faces.

People ate the afternoon meal that preceded the holiday quickly, near the trees. Bronscha served the old men vegetable soup and chunks of corn pie. Avraham Yitzhak ran wild between the wagons, completely disregarding her threats.

The old men ate without speaking. On Sabbath eve and even more so on the eve of holy days such as Rosh Hashanah, they would speak very little, their gestures sparing, and neither accept other people's help nor ask for anything for themselves. If someone approached them and asked something, they would respond with only a word or two or with pursed lips. Among the old men there are some who will occasionally undertake a fast of the spoken word. Once, Old Yerachmiel vowed not to let a single word pass his lips until we reached Jerusalem. His life in the camp was a mute one. Were it not for his prayers, mainly whispered, his existence would have been even more restricted. His prayers connected him to the world and to the Creator of the World. No one knew what transpired in his soul or what he was thinking. Sometimes it seemed to me that there was a cloud about his neck. He would be the first to arrive at morning prayers. On the Sabbath and on holy days, he would sometimes lead the prayers.

On the eve of the holiday the old men put on their white clothes. They encircled the table on which the Torah lay and then sat in the first row. The dealers sat behind them, and the wagon drivers stood. Truth be told, that was how it was every year. But this time, they brought Ephraim on his pallet, wrapped in a yellowed prayer shawl, and they placed him next to the table. One of the old men handed him a holiday prayer book. Ephraim took the prayer book in his hands and kissed it. Old Yerachmiel led the prayers quietly, in a restrained manner. But in the midst of the prayers there unexpectedly crept into his voice a tone that was not so much one of reciting prayers but of reckoning sums, as if he were not a leader of prayers but a keeper of accounts. Alarmed, I closed my eyes.

After the prayers, my teacher, Old Avraham, delivered the sermon. He spoke of the hard days that lay ahead of us and immediately added that we, thank God, were well protected and had nothing to fear because the God of Israel would lead us triumphantly into our land and our city, and that every tribulation that befell us had a purpose. If we could overcome our carelessness and false illusions, no harm would befall us because God was watching over our convoy, just as He had in the desert watched over those who had departed from Egypt.

This time Old Avraham didn't reproach us or stir us up, and he didn't quote accusatory biblical verses. He treated us as if we were sick people who needed to be wrapped in soft blankets, and not a herd of sinners. After he finished speaking, Ephraim was taken back to his place in the wagon, and the clearing suddenly emptied out. One of the old men, one of those you hardly noticed, lifted his head out of his prayer shawl, looked around him, and said, "We've passed through the corridor, and now it's time to prepare for the living room." His gaze was full of wonder at how swiftly life had gone by.

Later, a brawl broke out among the wagon drivers. Shimkeh and Chiyuk had not taken part in the prayers and were drunk. In their drunkenness, they had for some reason blessed those returning with new year's greetings. On hearing their blessing, one of the wagon drivers upbraided them and called them "filthy." His words ignited Chiyuk's ire, and the flames spread, engulfing everyone. The old men hurried over to put them out. When their pleas had no effect, they wedged themselves between the opponents to separate them.

The holidays are sometimes disrupted in this way, but this time it was a bitter brawl. Many faces were scratched, and neither requests nor entreaties were of any help. Even after the brawl, curses continued to fly.

"Almighty God!" cried out one of the old men. "What is happening to us? Why are we Jews desecrating this holy day? We have just one Rosh Hashanah; it is unique among all other days. How can seeing eyes be so blind?"

32

Between Rosh Hashanah and Yom Kippur heavy rains fell, and everyone was busy stretching out the tarpaulins and repairing the tears. The tent that the wagon drivers had put up collapsed upon itself. People crammed into the covered wagons and dared not venture out. This had happened before, but this year there was a feeling that the pursuers who were always pushing us into dire straits were actually getting nearer. The old men prayed, studied sacred texts, and recited penitential prayers, while everyone else played cards or reminisced. Sruel told me about his elderly mother and father, who had made a great effort to keep visiting him in jail. The visits were held behind bars and were wordless because of his mother's weeping. During their first few visits his father had been angry, but eventually he grew indifferent to his wife's crying and sat beside her in silence.

"Don't come," Sruel would implore, but they wouldn't listen to his pleas and kept coming back. Their visits pained him more than the beatings. Finally they stopped coming, but they continued to send him clothes and dried fruit.

"Do you remember them clearly?" I asked for some reason.

"No. At one time I did, but now they seem like shadows to

me. I can't even remember a word they said. It's my fault. I should have been able to keep them in memory."

Years later, his elder brother, a tall and sickly man, came to visit him. Sruel was brought before him. The brother immediately informed him that it was their parents' idea for him to come, not his. As is customary, Sruel said, "May God bless you." His brother rebuked him for this blessing and called him a scoundrel. Sruel became enraged and shouted at him. The jailers quickly took Sruel back to his cell, and so ended that brief, strange visit.

Sometime later Sruel learned that his brother had lost his mind and had been sent to an asylum on the outskirts of the city. Sruel learned of his death by chance. One of the jailers, who had worked as a guard at the asylum, told Sruel that his brother, in deep despair, had hung himself in the latrines.

"That's how it is," said Sruel, and he would say no more.

The rain fell incessantly. Sitting beneath the heavy tarpaulins, people recalled painful events from long ago, confessions and troubles that they had never before acknowledged. They recounted dreams and interpreted them. Ephraim, who had been in a state of deep slumber, awoke and spoke of the deserters who lie in wait for us on the road. This time he could describe them exactly: there were five, wearing the uniform of the Austrian army. Four lay in ambush and one kept lookout. When asked by one of the dealers if they were dangerous, he answered, "Yes."

Two days before Yom Kippur, the rains ceased and clear skies appeared above us. People brought out their cooking pots, made bonfires, and hung blankets and sheets on the branches of trees. The odor of mold, which had permeated the wagons, filled the open air. The women laundered and children ran around between the wagons.

In years past, at a time like this the old men would have climbed onto crates and poured out words of rebuke and conciliation. They would have asked for forgiveness and read Bible verses and excerpts from well-known holy books. This year they did this, too, but it was very different. No rebukes rent the air.

Itcheh Meir promised that from now on he would bind his arms with handcuffs, and as proof he displayed the handcuffs, which he had bought from one of the wagon drivers. At first, the wagon driver had refused to sell them, saying that they were as dear to him as his own hands, but Itcheh Meir offered him a fair price and the driver could not resist. In the past, at his behest, Itcheh Meir would be whipped by the old men on the eve of Yom Kippur. This time they refused.

"May the Almighty bless you from on high and may He help you." They blessed him and would say no more.

"Something has happened to us, hasn't it?" Sruel wondered.

"Nothing at all," I said for some reason.

"Nothing at all, you say? The old men are no longer angry. Am I wrong?"

"The rain has worn them out."

"From the rain, you say?"

Since Ploosh's death, Sruel has changed greatly. At first his hands shook with a nervous trembling, but now it seems as though he has calmed down. A frightening sort of wonderment radiates from his eyes. He rarely speaks and spends most of his time in deep contemplation. He can sit for hours on end without a sound escaping from his mouth. I do not dare to disturb his silences.

Sometimes Sruel would ask me to explain a word or a verse from the Bible. When I responded, the wonderment in his eyes became more intense. Once I read a passage from *The Path of the Just* to him.

"You read well," he said.

"Like anyone else."

"You love what's written."

His awe frightened me. This strong man, who once cast fear upon everyone but could just as easily be amiable and full of confidence—it was as if he had absorbed into his body all the softness and weakness of the old men.

"Don't forget the pail," he said. He never used to say "Don't forget."

Sruel was now extremely careful with the household items—two pots, two spoons, a few forks, a saltshaker, and a shopping basket—that he had inherited from the old men. After using them, he would wrap them in rags and hide them away in a chest.

The Prut is turbulent in these parts. It's hard to spread the nets, and whatever we bring up is inedible. We toss crabs and eels back into the churning waters and return empty-handed to the camp. Eventually, we decided to return to a place where we had already been. To our surprise, there we found plenty of carp. Sruel was happy, but his happiness was not as it had been before. At night, he has one drink too many and curls up under one of the wagons like a man trying to escape from his pursuers.

"Laishu, I'm afraid of the rains."

"We'll spread out the tarpaulins."

"The water still gets inside."

On Yom Kippur, Sruel wrapped himself in a prayer shawl and would not lift his head until the prayers had ended. I sat next to him and felt his body tremble. At the end of the fast, he was served a glass of tea and a slice of cake. His face was white and his eyes shone with a bitter soulfulness. Later, I brought him a bowl of fruit compote that had been handed out in the kitchen.

He grasped the bowl with both hands, as if I had brought him a gift from heaven.

As on every evening following Yom Kippur, some people ran away. We saw them fleeing, and not a single person tried to stop them. Lame Yekutiel was among them. Over the past year he had appeared in Pinchas's performances, and his voice had made a strong impression.

Those who ran away were nimble, and in his effort to catch up with them, Yekutiel hopped on his healthy leg. Sometimes, a man's escape is more vividly etched in our memories than the time he spent with us. But Yekutiel will always be remembered, for he was an excellent chess player. Among the dealers there were some excellent players, but he surpassed them all. Had he invested his talents in the Talmud, he would have been an outstanding scholar. But what can one do? In his world there was room for nothing but the chessboard. Now, when I close my eyes, I can see him leaning on the board, a malicious delight flickering in his eyes, for he has grasped all his opponent's vulnerabilities, and in a moment he will unleash the knights and the pawns onto the undefended fields. His opponent will have no choice but to throw up his hands, acknowledging defeat.

33

At the end of Yom Kippur, right after the meal that broke the fast, the wagon drivers went to build the sukkah. The fast had not affected them. They worked energetically, sawing large beams and joining slender planks to them. Within an hour, the frame of a sukkah stood in the clearing. They immediately set up the benches and covered the roof with loose branches. As soon as the work was done, the women served them mugs of coffee and cookies, and they ate and drank and gazed with satisfaction at their handiwork.

It's hard to sleep after the fast. The musicians took up their instruments and held them close. They played old melodies, melodies that they had picked up on the road, and a few of their own. As if by magic, these sounds evoked distant places and years past. And what prayers had not accomplished, their playing did: people burst into tears, as if they had just been told that they would never regain what they'd had and that the future would not be bright.

The old men are weak but not depressed. They look like people who have accomplished what they were given to do, and now, with a wordless gesture, they entrust their lives to the Creator of the World, to do with them as He pleases. Later, they sat and read from the Zohar. Whenever they read from

the Zohar, they send me away. I once opened the book, immediately saw that its letters were unlike those in other holy
books, and closed it. There are many secrets in the Torah, but I
am not yet worthy of them.

The following day, a huge crowd of peasants gathered
around us. They had discovered that we were on a pilgrimage
to Jerusalem and had come to see this marvel with their own
eyes. They were short, wore long smocks, and their faces displayed an old-fashioned reverence for heaven. They had previously come across Jewish peddlers, but never Jews on their way
to Jerusalem. We bought cornmeal, potatoes, and dried fruits
from them. Women brought their sick children to the old men
so that they could be blessed. The old men blessed them but
refused to accept money.

"The Jews are good. The Jews are generous," they said,
laying fruits and vegetables at the entrance of the sukkah and
repeatedly kissing the old men's hands.

Over the course of our travels we had come across many
peasants. Most attacked us, threw stones at us, or set their dogs
on us. These peasants were quiet. A kind of temperateness
infused their swarthy faces. They were in awe of us.

"Where are you traveling?" they asked in astonishment.

"Everything is in the hands of God," said the old men, and
this reply made them happy. Sruel spoke to them in their language, and they looked at him with admiration. As I have
already noted: people are reflected in his face. Good people
bring to the surface all the good that is hidden deep within
him. Angry people sadden him; his face darkens and he
escapes to the horses.

Now, some of the quietness and patience of these tillers of
the soil clung to him. He didn't speak to them using lofty
words and he didn't boast, as he sometimes would. Eventually,
one of the peasants turned to him.

"So, what kind of Jews are you?" he asked mockingly.

"Jews."

"Jews don't go on pilgrimages to Jerusalem."

"But you can see for yourselves that we're pilgrims."

"And how long will you stay in Jerusalem?" another peasant interrupted.

"Forever."

"You won't come back to us?"

"We have a saying that if someone goes to Jerusalem, he does not return."

"But who will ensure your livelihood?"

"God in heaven looks after all His creatures. He will take care of us."

Upon hearing Sruel's words, the peasant crossed himself.

On Sukkot the skies were clear and rain fell only at night. My teacher took me to his corner and we read the weekly Bible portion. His voice was soft and pleasant, and his age was hardly noticeable. Since he had stopped testing me on what I learned, I was much less anxious, and being near him moved me. That night he told me about the city of his birth, Shedlitz. He spoke with emotion, and it was clear that he felt attached to the part of the country where both he and his ancestors had been born. He didn't complain and didn't claim any wrongdoing, but spoke of his impoverished ancestors who had immersed themselves in the study of Torah and had built the house of study with their own hands. When he finished speaking, he drew an envelope out of his coat pocket.

"My dear Laishu," he said to me, "because no man knows when his time will come, I have written a short will. Do me the kindness of placing it in the lining of your coat. On the day that God gathers me to Him, open the envelope and do as I have requested within it."

"My teacher." The words trembled as I spoke them.

"We are commanded not to fear death. Death is nothing but an apparition. Today we are here, and tomorrow we are there."

He spoke quietly, as if he weren't giving me his will but making some trivial request. The envelope remained clasped in my hands; I was afraid to put it in the lining of my coat.

"Put the envelope in your lining and forget about it," he said, gazing at me with great compassion.

At that moment I knew that many scenes might be erased from my memory, but not this brief interchange. *My teacher,* I almost said, *God has to bring us to Jerusalem.* But I immediately understood that one does not say "has to" about God, and so I kept silent.

34

After that we made our way along the Prut without losing our way and without any delays. Were it not for Ephraim, who had stirred from his silence and again began speaking about the deserters, the blessing of the Days of Awe would have lingered with us. From day to day, Ephraim's madness seemed more alarming. When we didn't respond to his warnings, a hint of anger crept into his voice.

"Ephraim, enough!" a dealer rebuked him.

"I can't help it."

"But not aloud. There are woman and children among us."

"The deserters are ambushing us. If we don't rout them at the right time, they will rise early and kill us first. Don't you see them?"

"We don't see a thing."

"There are five of them, armed head to foot."

"We don't see a thing."

"If no one else sees them, if only I can see them, that's a sign that I must be wrong," Ephraim said and fell silent.

Ephraim had no idea to what extent he was right, although it was not his deserters who ambushed us, but the dreadful plague that had spared us over the High Holy Days. It now caught up with us, gripping us mercilessly in its talons.

At first it pounced on the children. The warm compresses were of no use, nor were the infusions of herbs that they were given to drink. Their screams rent the heavens every night.

The wagon drivers went to fetch a medic from the village. The medic, a tall, elderly peasant, immediately proclaimed that the children had typhoid and had to be isolated. The terror was as cold as ice. People kept their distance from one another and immersed their dishes and pots in boiling water. Fear is loathsome, and the fear of death is many times more loathsome. When they eventually fetched a doctor, there was nothing he could do but confirm that the children's situation was desperate and that he could do nothing to save them. One by one, the children fell silent and passed away. Among those who died was Bronscha's son, Avraham Yitzhak. Bronscha, who had never shown him any compassion and who would beat him mercilessly, now howled like a wounded animal, tearing out her hair and blaming herself for his death. There was no graveyard in the area, so we dragged ourselves through the marshes and the forest glades until we found one. The warden at the graveyard didn't look kindly on us and demanded a very high fee. This time, the committee didn't haggle; they paid. The burials went on until nightfall. They were hellish. It was impossible to tear the mothers away from their dead children.

Then came the long nights of bereavement. The bonfires burned throughout the night, and people surrounded the mothers with warm drinks and words. Whispered verses from the Bible and other sacred writings were heard everywhere, but they didn't sound like words of consolation. They sounded, instead, like restrained cries.

"If there's a God in the heaven, He should appear immediately!" one woman shouted in her sorrow. The old men tried to calm her down, but they only fanned the flames of her despair.

Panic set in after the death of the children, and some people fled the convoy. A few made off like thieves in the night, while others announced that they did not have the strength to bear it anymore: it would be better to die in an abandoned hospice than in a damp wagon.

Most embarrassing of all was how the Gold Man left. This dealer, who in more favorable times had risen a bit above himself and had distributed his plentiful money to the needy, leaving nothing for himself except for his own scant needs; this extraordinary man, who looked like a monk and was admired by many because he had taken upon himself strict vows of silence, suddenly rose and declared that he had no intention of becoming sick here and of being buried in one of those neglected graveyards, which were a disgrace to the Jewish people. He who had once been as silent as a stone got up and, in a strange outburst, spoke about the need to disperse and about the prohibition against deluding ourselves with empty visions. His bitterness was sharp and well articulated, and his words gushed over us like boiling water. One of the drivers—one of the coarser ones—who found the Gold Man's words particularly grating, called out in a slurred voice, "Go, already! Go!"

"There's no need to drive me away. I'm going anyway."

"But cut the talk!"

"You're not going to prevent me from speaking the truth!"

"Leave! Or I'll beat you."

"I'm not afraid."

"Don't provoke me."

But the Gold Man drew back and didn't continue speaking. He picked himself up and went on his way, as though reclaiming what he had given away.

35

From there the horses raced on, going faster and faster. It seemed to us that if we only galloped along quickly, the plague would not catch up with us. Fortunately, the skies favored us, the peasants and the gendarmes did not attack us, and those in whose power it was to give were not stingy. Where we had made camp our musicians entertained the villagers, who paid generously. There weren't many Jews in this district, and the few who were there didn't look like Jews. They weren't happy to see us; they were afraid and ashamed, and shut themselves away in their homes.

But in the end, even that wild gallop could not save us. Two of the old men came down with typhoid and were snatched away, just hours apart. The dead were laid out, but we didn't know where to bury them. We retraced our steps and searched for a graveyard. The search lasted for two days, and when we at last found a small, neglected graveyard, the warden demanded a huge sum of money for the graves. The old men's entreaties were to no avail. The warden stood his ground and refused to open the gate. Left with no other option, two wagon drivers finally approached the warden and, without standing on ceremony, told him that if he refused to open the gate, his end would be quite bitter. The man got scared, took a few spades and hoes out of his storeroom, and opened the room where the corpses were washed.

"Do what you have to do," he said in a frightened voice. "I've done my bit."

The wagon drivers dug the graves while the old men washed and prepared the bodies, and thus we gave them a Jewish burial.

After the burial we said the afternoon prayers alongside the wagons. The warden joined the group and prayed without swaying, like a non-Jew. At the end of the prayers, one of the dealers asked him, "What's the name of this place?"

The warden smiled mockingly and said, "This is a graveyard and that's my hut."

"Are there any villages around here?"

"This is marshland and ground that's no good for anything."

"And what became of the Jews here?"

"They were killed," he said, and one could see that this remote tragedy no longer pained him. His face was covered with scars that bore stark witness to the fact that life itself is stronger than anything else. You could be killed seven times and still return to life.

"I also had a family once," said the warden with a foolish smile.

"And what happened to them?" the dealer asked.

It appeared as though the warden did not understand his question.

"I'm not complaining," he said. "I have a home, a garden, and fruit trees. When there's a funeral, people drop a few coins into the box. A man needs nothing more." His hands bore witness to the fact that he knew how to hold a hoe and a shovel, and if it was necessary to beat a rebellious animal, he would.

"So you're on a pilgrimage to the Holy Land?" he asked with the cunning of a peasant.

"We are." The dealer was terse.

"And how long have you been on the road?"

"A long time. Too long."

"And you're not afraid of the sea?"

"No."

The warden asked nothing else and retired to the fore-court of the graveyard. But before he turned to go into his hut, he waved and drew two iron bars across the gates. The wooden doors momentarily buckled under the weight of the metal, then straightened themselves.

It was already night. We settled the wagons not far from the graveyard. People lit bonfires and prepared coffee. As after every funeral, this time, too, grief was mixed with a selfish satisfaction that we were still alive. I have noticed that the barrier between the living and the dead rises quickly. We buried the dead and immediately began to prepare coffee for the mourners. The aroma of the coffee gave us a thirst for strong liquor.

Later, two dealers scaled the fence, knocked on the door of the warden's hut, and asked to buy cornmeal from him. At first he refused, but when he saw that there were banknotes in the dealers' hands, he agreed. The women immediately set to preparing corn pie for the hungry crowd.

After the meal, the men rolled cigarettes and sat and smoked. Were it not for the darkness, I would have written down the names of those who had passed away. I'm scrupulous about writing down the names of the dead. Old Ya'akov, the man who left me the notebook, recently came to me in a dream and rebuked me for not immediately adding new names to the list. Since that dream, I've been more careful about keeping it. When I read the names of the dead, I recall their faces and the look of the places where they were buried. I feel that these years have been solidly planted within me, and that I'll be with the convoy for the rest of my life. Sometimes, it seems to me that those who have died and those who have fled haven't really departed from us, but are waiting somewhere down the road so that they can rejoin us. In a dream, I once saw Mamshe and Maya chatting away like sisters. Maya told Mamshe a joke and Mamshe laughed riotously. It seems to me that even Ploosh has not relinquished his place in the convoy. The convoy is, indeed, dwindling from week to week, but anyone who has ever been a part of it will yearn for it forever.

36

After the death of the two old men, we advanced much more slowly. The rain fell incessantly, and the roads were impassable. We were forced from our path as we had to stock up on water and basic necessities. Yet we didn't remain in one place. In prior times the old men would complain about the delays, grumbling and casting blame. Now they are resigned to the delays. The dealers, their former enemies, have changed more than any of us. Although they continued to trade, and a few of them would disappear for a day or two to change money or buy a garment, there was no zest in what they did. It was obvious that their imagination, which had previously pulled them along with enchanted rope, had dimmed. They were no longer as nimble as they had once been. Occasionally, you'd find a dealer sitting on the riverbank lost in his daydreams, like a drunk. In their favor, let it be said that they didn't impose their suffering on the others; they didn't behave in a miserly way. On the contrary, a heartfelt generosity, which we had never seen before, radiated from them. It was as if they had acknowledged that their days in this world were numbered and that it would be better for them if they were good and helped others. Only Salo, one of the most childlike among them, would buzz about like a sick bee. "I don't know what's going to be. I'm afraid of autumn."

His childishness touched my heart. There are people among us who are wise and wily, there are vulgar and threatening creatures, but there are also a few naive ones. Salo, who all the days of his life had been a dealer and had traded wisely, remained a child. Naturally, the children loved him. He would play with them and make funny noises for them. Their death wounded him terribly; you would sometimes find him sitting alone and mumbling to himself, "They are no longer. They're in heaven."

"It's forbidden to mourn to excess." The old men reproached him.

"I loved them."

Salo, a happy, easygoing man who was drawn to the crushed of spirit among us, became a shadow of his former self. He began to age prematurely, and his fingers shook from anxiety. The slightest noise would frighten him. He would wake up at night crying out, "Avraham Yitzhak, where are you?" He had loved Avraham Yitzhak greatly, and after his death he would call out to him at night in a voice that sounded like the howling of a jackal.

One evening he went up to one of the old men.

"I'm afraid of the journey," he confessed.

The old man's response was swift. "Is it only the journey that you're afraid of?"

Salo was shocked by the old man's answer. "What can I do?" he muttered.

"You should fear the Creator of the World, not the journey."

"Not be afraid?"

"Why are you asking, since you already know?"

Salo stood where he was as if he had been slapped. It seemed to me that he was about to cover his face and burst into tears. Later on, without any apparent connection, he did burst into tears. From far off, Sruel noticed and went over to him.

"Why are you crying, Salo?" he asked kindly.

"I'm afraid."

"What are you afraid of?"

"I don't know."

"We are nearing the sea, and from there we'll go to the Land of Israel."

"So we won't die on the way?"

"What are you saying!"

"Are you sure?"

"No doubt about it."

After Salo had calmed down, he told Sruel that from time to time he thought of returning home to say good-bye to his mother, as he had not properly taken leave of her. If the truth be told, he had not disclosed to her that he was going to the Land of Israel. But he didn't have the courage to return, because he feared he would no longer find her alive.

"I should flog myself because I have no courage."

"Don't worry, in the Land of Israel everything will be set to rights."

"I just don't have the courage."

"What was, was. Right now we should be worrying about the days ahead of us." Sruel spoke to him in a practical, fatherly tone. The wagon drivers sometimes mock Salo, and a few jokes about him have gone around. But now everyone tries to distract him, promising him that everything will be different in the Land of Israel.

37

And then the inevitable came to pass. The skies changed, and low clouds approaching from the south darkened the light of day all at once. We were in the very heart of the plain, and we tried to escape from this open trap. The wagon drivers lashed the horses mercilessly, and the horses reared as if fire gripped them in its talons. Furious rain showers scourged and suffocated us as we cowered under the tarpaulins. It was clear that this was only the beginning of our calamities and that what was to come would be many times worse. But we deluded ourselves into believing that salvation was at hand. Ephraim had implanted this delusion within us. He had seen visions of a warm Jewish village that would happily and hospitably provide us with shelter and would give us not only hot food but dry clothes, too.

This illusion swept through us the following day as well, although the horses no longer galloped. They could hardly pull the wagons out of the mud. *Almighty God, give us some place of refuge,* the old men prayed aloud, and everyone joined in their prayers.

Meanwhile, the waters rose all over. The Prut overflowed its banks, and we plodded on, lost in the wet darkness. The wagon drivers did what they could: they beat the horses cruelly, and the wagons shook with recurring jolts. Finally, they threw up their hands and said, "It's no longer in our control."

After days of lurching and jostling, we reached an abandoned flour mill. It was built of bricks, but the roof covered only the sides. The wagon drivers removed the tarpaulins, but no one moved. It was as if everyone had been struck dumb, including me.

What took place during the following days was unlike anything I had ever seen. Vistas of red filled my head and shook my temples. I was crawling inside a narrow tunnel, choking with heat and thirst, struck with blindness.

In this conflagration I saw my mother and father as I had never seen them before: they were walking hand in hand inside an illuminated tunnel, but not in my direction. I tried to shout, but my voice became choked. I also saw Mamshe. Her face was clear, as if the madness had fallen from her eyes and only a pale strip of grief still flickered on her brow. She contemplated me with an unpleasant stare and said, "What are you doing here?"

Amid the shooting flames, I saw the holy books that I had studied with my teacher—*The Path of the Just, Duties of the Heart,* and *The Guiding Lamp.* My teacher was sitting crosslegged, his coat burning, but his face showed no sign of panic; it was as if he were raised aloft, living detached from us.

How many days I burned with fever, I will never know. When I opened my eyes, I saw Sruel, the falcon on his shoulder, and I immediately understood that the deluge had subsided. Sruel was as happy to see me as if I had returned to him from the dead. During the days that I hadn't seen him, Sruel had changed greatly. His beard had grown wild, and he looked like a wretched peasant whose herd had been ravaged by foot-and-mouth disease. He immediately told me that only he, Shimkeh, and Chiyuk were still on their feet; all the others lay prostrate in the wagons, burning up with fever.

When I opened my eyes the following day, I saw the three of them standing over me. Sruel wet my mouth with some liquid. The liquid touched my lips and seeped into me. Now Sruel looked like one of the dealers, not especially strong, perhaps because he was wearing faded and patched overalls. Shimkeh and Chiyuk stood at his side like two tired and submissive beadles.

"How do you feel?" Sruel asked.

"Red," I said, and I immediately understood that I hadn't used the right word.

Later, I felt as if I were floating, and black water was pulling me down into a whirlpool. I knew that I must not close my eyes, and I didn't close them. Unexpected groans and shards of words came out of the wagons. From my corner I could see pale arms, outstretched, pleading for water.

"What happened?" I asked Sruel.

"You're better now."

Then I apparently asked something that I should not have, because the three of them came closer and glared at me. I wanted to apologize, but the words vanished from my mouth. The men knelt at my side, and Sruel spoke to me using complicated words that I didn't understand. I couldn't overcome my weakness, and I closed my eyes.

Within me now burned a fevered mixture of the banks of the Prut, the cornfields where I had been put to work like a slave, and the dark streets. It was suddenly clear to me that I would have to give a reckoning for all my actions. I wanted to get up and go over to Blind Menachem and ask for his forgiveness, but my body was as heavy as lead and it stuck to the ground.

The following day, the pains in my body subsided and I felt a slight relief, as if I had been tossed up from churning waters. Sruel sat beside me and fed me some watery gruel. His eyes were red, and it was obvious that he was greatly weakened. I didn't dare ask who was alive and who had abandoned us. Shimkeh and Chiyuk never stirred from the wagons. With trembling hands they brought liquids to the mouths of those who were sick. Now I saw that the horses had been released from their harnesses and were grazing in a ditch. Ephraim's head hovered over me from his wagon, as if it had been detached from his body.

Sruel brought me gruel in the evening, too. I was hungry and I gulped down the warm liquid. For some reason I asked why the falcon was late in returning, and Sruel replied that it would alight any minute. And so it did. I remembered how once, one of the old men had warned Sruel that it was forbidden for him, a Jew, to form such close ties with winged creatures. To prove it, he cited two verses from the Bible. Sruel, who hadn't understood the verses, said, "What can I do? I didn't go to him, he came to me."

This answer had surprised the old man and he said, "Be that as it may."

After that conversation, Sruel treated the falcon differently. Although he didn't drive it away, he didn't show it the affection he had shown it earlier. The falcon sensed Sruel's standoffishness and made many graceful swooping motions to endear itself to him. In time, the old man's warning was erased from Sruel's heart, and he went back to loving the wondrous creature that clung to him.

"Sruel," I said.

"What do you want, dear boy?"

"Have the waters receded?" I asked, just as my teacher once asked.

"I don't understand you," said Sruel, and he chuckled. His laughter exposed his tired face and all the goodness hidden inside it.

38

It was only the following day that I learned how close I had really been to being with my mother and my father. I wanted to remember that brief touch, but the feeling eluded me and faded. Sruel brought me a bowl of gruel and a cup of tea. His expression was full of forgiveness, and I saw how utterly selfless his devotion to the sick was. Shimkeh and Chiyuk, who had never taken part in the prayers, now seemed like two pious Jews in later life. Their hard years in jail could not be seen in their bearing. They cared for the sick devotedly, like servants who had learned to love their labor.

To my surprise, the first to raise himself up a bit and show some signs of life was Ephraim. "Thank you, Sruel," he called out to Sruel, who had brought him a bowl of gruel. His face was pale, and a wonderment glowed in his eyes.

"Good to see you, Ephraim." The words slipped out of me.

"Who is it?" he said with surprise.

"It's me, Laish. I feel better."

"Me, too."

"What happened to us?" I asked like a simpleton.

"We got sick. You don't know that we got sick?"

Perhaps because of the peaked cap that he wore on his head, Ephraim looked happy that he was still alive. I was also happy to be alive. People go through the torments of sickness, and then they are spared—and alive.

"Did they also bring you gruel?" Ephraim asked in a childlike voice.

"Sruel brought me some excellent gruel," I replied immediately, and the memory of its pleasant warmth again sweetened my lips.

Evening came, and the blue lights of the night shone coolly. Two large bonfires burned at the entrance to the mill, but their warmth could not be felt. I felt that the last few days had given us a cruel kneading. Whoever survived would never be the same. Shimkeh and Chiyuk were different, too. For now, at least, they were on their feet, taking quick swigs from their bottles and dashing from place to place. Sruel told them what to do and they were as obedient as day laborers, at the same time growling, "What's past is gone."

That night we learned that Bronscha had passed away. That strong and bitter woman, who looked like a peasant and cursed like one, had succumbed. Since her return, she had become beloved by us all. Occasionally, a torrent of rage would gush out from within her, but mostly she was quiet and absorbed in her work—helping the old men without asking for payment. Now she, too, was in the World of Truth. From Sruel's expression, I learned that death had settled into every corner. Had Shimkeh and Chiyuk been less drunk, they would have been enlisted in the struggle against it, but in their unstable condition they could barely carry out small tasks. Sruel wasn't angry at them, but despair was chiseled into his face.

Most of the day the skies were clear and cold and the silence was thick. Had it not been for the groans of the horses, which were now tied up like prisoners, were it not for those dumb creatures, which would occasionally raise their heads up from the grass to let out a sorrowful neigh, the silence would have overwhelmed us. The bonfires burned without pause. Shimkeh or Chiyuk would come by every hour to toss a log or a bunch of twigs onto the piles, and the fires would flare up.

Sleep was as hard as sickness. Sruel tried giving water to those burning up with fever, but their heads would droop in his hands. Eventually, Sruel himself collapsed. Now the camp burned without anyone looking after it. Large stars hung low at night, illuminating the wagons. Sometimes a cry for help would come from the wagons, only to break off immediately. Shimkeh and Chiyuk were drunk, and they staggered about as if they were asleep. A few of the sick were very demanding, and they kept Shimkeh and Chiyuk constantly on their feet. But most of them were quiet, sunk within their illness.

One evening Ephraim lifted his head.

"Laish, can you hear me?" he cried out.

"I hear you."

"I wanted to tell you that I knew your parents well. They were decent and honest people."

"Why do you say decent and honest?" I made it hard going.

"Because some people did cast doubt on their good name. But you have nothing to worry about. They were decent and honest."

"What sort of doubt was cast on them?"

"They were—how can I say it?—they were unusual people."

"What's wrong with that, Ephraim?"

"They were different from the rest."

"Were they smugglers?"

"God forbid."

"What did they do?"

"They helped the poor, even poor peasants who were not of our people."

"And why did this give them a bad name?"

"Because they would organize strikes and demand justice for the poor. You have nothing to worry about. They were decent people. I don't know if I've done right by telling you. Last night I saw them in a dream. It's been years since I've seen them."

"Why didn't they join our convoy?"

"They were carried off by typhoid. Typhoid will carry us all off."

"Ephraim, I thank you for what you've told me."

"I'm not sure if I've done right by telling you. It seems that I needed to."

"I've always felt that something was not altogether right."

"Don't pay any attention to the slanderers. Your parents were decent, honest people and they helped all those who were wretched. They passed away on Hanukkah, on the day of the first candle. Both at the same time, I think. Don't forget to say Kaddish."

"Thank you, Ephraim, I won't forget."

"They called them Communists, but it doesn't matter."

39

Then I was overcome by a deep sleep. I was once again on the road alongside the Prut, but this time I was with my parents. They were wearing short coats and they stood at the doorway of a sawmill, arguing with the overseers. They looked thin beside the sturdy overseers. Almighty God, I said to myself, my parents fought for the downtrodden, and I worry only about myself. Anyone who worries only about himself has no divine spark within him. I must recover and regain my strength, and I must stand up for the weak. Only he who stands up for the rights of the weak will find redemption. There is no other redemption. That's how the words came out of my mouth. I knew these were not my words, and yet they rolled off my tongue as if they were.

When people awoke from their sleep, they were pale and gaunt, as if their flesh had been passed through a thresher. Hunger gaped from lifeless eyes. Even though they were drunk and woozy, Shimkeh and Chiyuk stood beside the large pots and served anyone who held out a bowl.

These were the same fields through which we had previously made our way, and yet they were different. The desolation stretched all the way to the horizon. The few trees were shriveled; their parched branches rustled dryly. The horses, who only a few days earlier had been whinnying lustily, now stood silently gazing at us with a heavy sadness.

Whoever had the strength to rise to his feet would go over to the bonfires. A few of the old men managed to overcome their weakness and climb down from the wagons. They held their frail hands out to the fire. I didn't move from Sruel's pallet. It was hard to believe that a man like Sruel could succumb like anyone else. I moistened his lips and prayed to God to speed his recovery. Without him, we would be lost.

At night, when everyone else was fast asleep, Shimkeh and Chiyuk would drag logs from the nearby woods and throw them onto the fire. The fire blazed throughout the night. I noticed that Shimkeh and Chiyuk had stopped speaking. They mumble, and fractured syllables come out instead. They've started calling me Vagadu. Their steps are as heavy as the logs that they drag, and their long coats make them seem short.

The days that followed were white and cold, and at night the bonfires gave off a harsh light. We drank tea and ate roasted potatoes. I would sit for hours staring at the horses and at Sruel's two emaciated dogs. Since his illness, they have lost their zest. They don't touch the food that I give them and spend most of the day curled up under Sruel's wagon. Whenever he coughs or sighs, they prick up their ears.

There was little talking. You could hear the fields breathe, the gurgling of the brooks, and the murmuring of the Prut. Sometimes a stray cow or a foal would wander over, gaze at us for a moment, and then flee. The winter light was thick, and it flowed beneath our feet slowly, like frozen water that had broken apart. Darkness came early; when it did, we would all collapse heavily into the jaws of sleep.

Ephraim began talking to me again about my parents. It must have troubled him because he again swore to me that my parents were honest and decent people and that anyone who had given them a bad name would not get off lightly. It was not for themselves that they had worked so hard, but for the sake of widows and orphans.

"Were they young?" I asked for some reason.

"They were very young," Ephraim was quick to reply.

Peasants arrived from neighboring villages and spread their wares on the ground. Anyone who could summon the strength to drag his legs would go over to them and buy something. Shimkeh and Chiyuk bought dried fruits for the old men and vodka for themselves. They drank nonstop, and their drunkenness made us dizzy. It was hard to stand on one's legs, but even harder still to lie on the hard bedding.

Between the first light of day and the dark of night, several images appeared to me: Sruel's falcon did not stir from his side. Sruel drove him away, but the bird was not deterred and returned to him. Ephraim spoke to Shimkeh and to Chiyuk as if they hadn't beaten him, as if they were his childhood friends. Shimkeh and Chiyuk did all the work without saying anything, but occasionally a wave of anger surged out of them, and they fell upon the tethered horses and beat them.

My teacher, Old Avraham, opened his eyes wide and called out, "Laish!" In my excitement I wanted to say a blessing, but the words had left my mouth. I moistened his forehead with water and immediately saw that he had spent many days struggling with the Angel of Death. His face was scratched and two wounds festered on his neck.

Death, I felt, no longer clung to us, but hovered over us. *Giving charity saves you from death!* I remember the rattling of the charity boxes at the entrances to the graveyards. Now there is no need to pile on entreaties. The dealers give charity generously, as if they finally understand that life is short and that it's best to dispense with money at the right time.

Tzilla has risen to her feet and stands at the stove cooking soup in large pots. Since Bronscha's death, she has taken her place. It's hard for her to stand and so she leans against the railing of one of the wagons. A blind old man, Yosef Haim, is trying to revive the prayer group. The old men find it hard to climb off the wagons. Even though he is barely steady on his feet, Yosef Haim manages the impossible and brings his friends tea or gruel, entreating them to rise for the prayer group. It seems to me, too, that if we begin the day with prayer, we will regain our strength and be back on our feet. A life without prayer is meaningless. Before I fall asleep, I recite the prayers that I remember by heart. But it's hard to pray without a prayer group. Prayer without a minyan has no wings; it sinks down to the lower depths.

The big secret, the secret surrounding those who are missing and have died, Shimkeh and Chiyuk carry within themselves. During the past weeks many have passed away. The wagons have emptied out, and loosened knapsacks and parcels are strewn alongside the wagons. Clothes that once covered people lie torn and shameful on the ground. Shimkeh and Chiyuk were the sole witnesses to the disappearances. Who knows the fate of these people? If Shimkeh is asked where the missing have gone, he waves his hand as if he were about to bring down a horsewhip on a rebellious animal and spits to the side.

40

Then the cold became very fierce, and those who could drag themselves to the forest and gather firewood got up and staggered over. The bonfires blazed, but they were barely able to warm the hands that stretched out toward them. We bought strips of cured leather from the peasants and wrapped them around the frozen legs of the old men.

"We'll die in this wasteland. They did well, those who ran away," one dealer grumbled to himself. But I was sure that this time, too, I would be saved. Since Old Yehezkiel had blessed me, his blessing protected me, and I knew that whatever danger threatened us would not touch me.

Meanwhile, peasants from the surrounding area brought their sick to the old men. The old men overcame their own weakness to get up and bless them. The peasants have a deep-seated faith in our old men. The old men lay their pale hands on the heads of the sick children while the children scream loudly.

My teacher, Old Avraham, opened his eyes again to ask how Ephraim was. I told him. I was afraid that he would ask about the others. Shimkeh and Chiyuk have kept secret the whereabouts of the many who have disappeared, and will reveal nothing to anyone. It may be that they themselves don't know too much; they have been wallowing in drunkenness for weeks. My teacher discussed with me the verse *The heavens are the Lord's, and the earth He has given to mankind.* He warned me against asking too much, since questions are the province of Satan. Satan pretends to be an innocent questioner, but in truth his intention is to ensnare you. After every attempt, one must devote oneself to prayer. Were it not for prayer, we would be exposed to every misfortune. My teacher already told me these things more than once, but now his words carry a new power.

Then our wagons were beset by unfamiliar creatures: a few village thieves and two wounded soldiers. Previously, they would never have dared to approach us, but now that our wagon drivers were also sick, they rummaged through the knapsacks and parcels that lay alongside the wagons.

"Send them on their way," Sruel ordered. But Shimkeh and Chiyuk, who usually do his bidding, made dismissive gestures, as if to say, *What does it matter?* Eventually, Sruel raised his voice and chased them away.

Jews do not inhabit this desolate region. But yesterday, a Jewish peddler arrived, and when he heard that we were journeying to Jerusalem, his eyes opened wide in alarm.

"Don't do this," he said.

"Why?" Sruel asked.

"Because the road is dangerous."

"In Galacz you get on a ship that brings you straight to the Land of Israel. Didn't you know?"

"The sea is the most dangerous."

"We aren't afraid."

Apparently the peddler didn't expect to get such a response and was taken aback.

"If only I had some of your faith," he said after a while.

"Here there are no Jews. All the Jews have fled this place; I'm all alone here."

"What are you afraid of?" Sruel lifted his hands.

"Everything," said the peddler with a tearful smile.

"By us it is written, *'You must not be afraid.'* If it's so written, that means there must be something to it."

"But I'm afraid all the same. The nights are the most frightening for me."

"You mustn't be afraid. Fear is a great sin."

"What should I do to overcome the fear?"

"Say *'The Lord is our God'* three times a day."

"That will uproot the fear from my heart?"

"Without a doubt."

"I'll try," he said and went on his way.

The peddler's expression remains with me. Some expressions can be harder than words. Words can be revoked, but a fixed gaze seeps into you like poison. I once heard my teacher say, "Lower your gaze and don't stare." Now I know what he meant. Even Ploosh the Cruel was sensitive to people's glances. If he ever sensed someone staring at him, he would raise his head and shout, "Take your eyes off me!"

Meanwhile, Shimkeh and Chiyuk have adopted a new habit, a frightening habit. At night they take Ploosh's revolver out of its hiding place, fire it into the air, and shout. Sruel, who has the power to make them do his bidding, doesn't stop them.

"Let them amuse themselves a bit. They work hard all the time," says Sruel, and he laughs at the strange sight of them in their long coats.

41

Shortly thereafter we sold three wagons and six horses, as well as the belongings left behind by those who had disappeared and those who had fled. The sale was swift and successful, but we felt like thieves. Sruel returned and downed a few glasses. Then he stood there giving people encouragement and promising that everything was for the best. Now we were lighter and the road to Jerusalem was open. But no one paid any attention to what he was saying. Shimkeh and Chiyuk sat hunched over the bonfire. People didn't remember their devotion and didn't come over to thank them. Surprisingly, they weren't annoyed at this ingratitude. They wallowed in their drunkenness, their faces closed and expressionless.

We set off without saying prayers. The old men sat in the first wagon. Very few were left. The wind was strong, but the tarpaulins protected us and the usual stuffiness prevailed inside. Before we left, the old men tried to find out where the dead had been buried. They pleaded with Shimkeh and Chiyuk to show them the graves. Evasive at first, Shimkeh and Chiyuk eventually claimed that no one aside from Bronscha had passed away, that everyone else had escaped. The old men didn't believe them. Shimkeh raised his hands and cried out, "We did the best we could; don't come complaining to us."

Menachem keeps asking if we have not lost our way, and Sruel promises him that the Prut is our guide; just as the Prut strives to reach the sea, so do we. Since Menachem rose from his sickbed he has been filled with anxiety, and he's once again afraid that one night he will be thrown off the wagon. Everyone has tried to convince him otherwise, but his fear is stronger than he is. Whenever the wagon stops he asks, "Where are we?" as if there were names to the places here.

At night we stop and light bonfires. Tzilla cooks soup for all of us. We are so few, hardly twenty men, barely two prayer groups, and the thick darkness that surrounds us is frightening. Our ranks have greatly thinned, and we now huddle alongside the old men who have survived.

After prayers, the old men gather around Ephraim's pallet and ask how he's feeling. He's embarrassed. He apologizes and says that soon he will be on his feet and will no longer be a burden. The old men soothe him with affectionate words. He doesn't speak about his pain. Once a day they remove his shirt and rub into his wounds ointment that we bought from the peasants. It doesn't seem as though his wounds have started to heal.

One evening, while we were still seated around the bonfire and trying to soak up the warmth, one of the wagon drivers got up. Without any warning, and in a voice that without any doubt was his own voice, he said, "I'm off."

"Where?"

"I'm going back home."

Sruel went over to him. "What's got into you?"

"I've wandered around enough; a man has to return home."

"What wrong have we done you?"

"Nothing, but I must return home. That's all." The wagon driver spoke in a forceful tone of voice.

"What home are you talking about? This is your home. We are your home."

"And don't I have a home in Pietrikov?"

"Your home in Pietrikov was burned down, dear fellow. You must get that house out of your head."

"That's true, you're right."

"We are going straight from here to Galacz. By Hanukkah, God willing, we will be in Jerusalem. It will have been worth it, believe me. There are things for whose sake life is worth living. I wouldn't give up on our convoy for anything."

"Why did I feel that I had to return to Pietrikov?"

"It was a mistake. Our feelings can mislead us. What's back there for us? Only troubles."

"You say that there's no point in returning home?"

"That's just what I'm saying, because this is our home and we have no other."

"How strange," said the wagon driver, and his large, crude features took on the sorrowful expression of a beast of burden.

That night the wagon drivers drank themselves into drunkenness. Sruel spoke at length about the need for courage and for preparation for the journey's end, because that would be our true test. Since his recovery from the epidemic, Sruel has become extremely thin, but he does not appear to be weak. He speaks fervently, spurring people to action. The wagon drivers do his bidding, and everyone hangs on his words. The convoy, if the truth be told, moves forward according to Sruel's moods. When he's sad, his sadness weighs down on us, but when he's fired by enthusiasm—and he usually is full of enthusiasm—he'll climb onto a crate and call out, "Jews, redemption is at hand! Don't be lazy!" Standing on a crate, he's like a hooligan who incites the village against the owners of the estate, full of power and belief. As for the wagon driver who wanted to return to his hometown, he walked about for several days wrapped in his coat and without uttering a word. In vain did people try to influence him. His longings, or whatever it was that he felt, must have driven him mad. One evening, without saying a word, he turned toward the Prut and jumped in. Everyone saw him jump, but no one was able to save him. The river seethed like the mythical Sambatyon.

42

Even we did not know how close we were to Galacz. The following day, we stood at its gates. It was morning, and the streets were packed with carriages and wagons. Galacz was a city like any other, but for some reason the facades of the buildings seemed darker. In jest, Sruel called out in Ruthenian, "Make way for pilgrims!" We made slow progress, and our ears picked out the jumble of languages: Romanian, Turkish, and Ruthenian. Everyone seemed to be streaming toward the port, yet the streets were too narrow to accommodate the throngs. But our wagon drivers were a step ahead: they turned onto the side streets and bypassed the traffic. Not an hour had passed, and we saw the water.

"There's more to go, but we'll make it shorter," called Sruel. Over the past few days he had been overflowing with faith and confidence, and if anyone complained or became depressed, Sruel would call out in contrast, "Remember, there's no God like ours."

We went from one alley to the next. The Jews were fleet of foot: the money changers and the middlemen scurried from doorway to doorway. After the days we spent being so close to death, the haste of these people seemed a little ridiculous.

We bought fresh bread, sheep's cheese, and pickles. The

hunger that had seized us as we began to recover was still plaguing us. We ate whatever we could lay our hands on, but we never felt full. Itcheh Meir no longer stole clothes, but loaves of bread and sausages.

"Where are you going?" a stall owner asked.

"To Jerusalem."

This holy name makes no impression here. Everyone knows that old Jews travel to Jerusalem, but sturdy ones like Sruel—why would they travel there? Sruel says jokingly that one hour in Jerusalem is worth seven years in Galacz. The dealers here are practical creatures, and if neither money nor something valuable is involved, they are not interested. And the Jews here, even though they speak Yiddish, do not resemble Jews.

Shimkeh and Chiyuk now look after my teacher, Old Avraham, because all the cash that we had been given for the wagons and the horses was sewn into his coat. My teacher has grown weaker, but his eyesight is undimmed, and whenever a money changer or middleman pounces on us, he tugs at my sleeve and says, "Come hear this rogue. Listen to how he tries to fool people."

Toward evening we found a large deserted area and halted the wagons. Shimkeh and Chiyuk brought firewood, and Tzilla started a fire, put a pot over it, and began preparing supper. Tzilla's cooking had the taste of home. And now that sheep's cheese was added to the potatoes, our appetite was boundless. Tzilla wasn't stingy and served more to anyone who wanted it.

There were only a few of us left. Yesterday our musical trio fled. I saw them sneaking away, crouching like thieves. As it turned out, everyone had seen them, but no one shouted at them to come back. They ran toward the water and hid beneath some willow trees. Shimkeh, who was sitting on the ground and eating his meal, said, "Our trio has run away. Shame on them; I'm not going to run after them."

Chiyuk was blunter.

"I'm not going to miss them," he said. "Lately, the way they've played only made me feel gloomy."

"Don't blame them," said Shimkeh, "they're afraid of Jerusalem."

"What's there to fear?"

"They're afraid that in Jerusalem they'll be brought to trial."

"I didn't hear them speak of it."

"That doesn't mean anything. Everyone's afraid of Jerusalem, but they don't dare to speak about it."

"I'm not afraid," said Chiyuk. "I've done what I've done and I've served my twenty-four years in jail. I've had what was coming to me."

"Murderers aren't liked anywhere, and in Jerusalem they'll be reminded of their evildoing morning and night."

"I'd tell them immediately what I've done and how many years I've served. You don't punish people twice."

"You're wrong."

"I'm not wrong. If anyone starts up with me, I'll thrash him."

"The Turks will put you straight into solitary. The Turks are crueler than the Romanians. They cut off thumbs."

"You only die once."

"That's true, but it isn't always easily."

"I'm going to die easily."

"How do you know?"

"I feel sure of it."

"Death can be very drawn out, with lots of suffering."

"Not for me."

"How come you're so sure?"

"I just am."

Sruel was busy chopping branches and I was sitting to one side, listening to Shimkeh and Chiyuk's conversation. Their

202 / Aharon Appelfeld

voices, unusual for them, were clear. Apparently death had preoccupied them for years, but until now they had never talked about it. While we were laying out the bedding and watering the horses, two thugs pounced upon my teacher. But Shimkeh and Chiyuk were quicker than they were. They grabbed the thugs and beat them mercilessly. There are thieves and rogues everywhere, but here they seem to swarm out of every corner. Sruel said something strange. "Everything is filthy except for Jerusalem."

It was a cold night, but no rain fell. Tzilla had bought excellent coffee from one of the dealers and prepared Turkish coffee and baked a cheesecake. Even though there were so few of us and we were weak and tired, we enjoyed the coffee and cake and the warmth of the bonfire. There was a feeling of closeness that brought other days to mind, days when we had been more numerous and more unified, the old men and the dealers occupied with their own concerns but not cut off from one another. The thought that our musical trio, whom we had loved so much, had abandoned us so close to the boat tightened our hearts and dampened our spirits.

43

The following day, in the half-light of early morning, we set out in the direction of the harbor. The wide wagons, which had once overflowed with people and packages, were jostled easily, and their emptiness echoed in the deserted streets. The water glittered from afar and long ships discharged black vapor.

"Laish, have you prayed already?" My teacher, Old Avraham, grasped my forearm.

"Not yet."

"What are you waiting for?"

"Perhaps we'll have a minyan."

"It is forbidden to depend on miracles."

Since the epidemic, we have not had a prayer group. My teacher has been trying in vain to bring the men together. Everyone is preoccupied by his own affairs. Even Ephraim, who used to pray devotedly, will only mutter a few blessings, as if he were discharging an obligation, and no more. It's hard to pray without a group. My teacher rebukes us again and again, saying that life without prayer reduces one to below the level of the beasts of the field, or even plants. Even animals and plants yearn for the Creator, and they express that yearning in their mooing and rustling.

"Life without yearning for God is a base life. Have pity on your life and pray," my teacher pleads.

Being jostled from place to place has not made old visions recede. Last evening the memory of Mamshe surfaced again. When we sold another two horses and two wagons, the buyer asked about the large cage and what it was for. Sruel, who conducted the negotiations, was embarrassed for a moment, but quickly rallied and said, "It's for sick animals or storage." The explanation seemed reasonable enough to the peasant, because he inquired no further.

Since Sruel spoke those words, it was as though Mamshe had come back to life. Last night they talked about her at length. Ephraim said that in the past few days he had seen her several times, and it appeared as though she were wandering about in the vicinity. Even though his visions have been shown to be false, they can still have an effect on us. Blind Menachem also heard her voice at night, and she was revealed to me in a dream, in the same green dress that she always wore, only more beautiful.

"There's no doubt," said Ephraim, "that if we manage to bring her to Jerusalem, she'll be healed." He told us how, many years ago, two people—a man and a woman—were sent to Jerusalem from his hometown. They had been crazy, and after a year came the good news that they had been healed.

We arrived at the coast by noon. It was a deserted strip of land, and all the debris of the port was littered along it. Some scrawny dogs who had found shelter in the garbage burst out of their den and fled. The coast was neglected, but the waters glittered dark blue. Several ships sailed by in the distance, and their elongated appearance made them seem huge. Ephraim was greatly moved by the sight; he stood up and recited a blessing.

The harbor itself was not far, but for some reason we didn't rush to get there. The winter sun was kind; it warmed us and dried our clothes a bit. Sruel took out the nets, and we immediately began to spread them out on the water. Handling the nets brought to mind the Prut's beautiful curves, its swiftly flowing waters, and the boulders that jut out like fearsome water creatures. The haul was not big, but it was enough for lunch.

"These are not like the fish of the Prut that melt in your mouth," said Shimkeh, and everyone agreed with him. Tzilla was happy that she had the provisions to prepare us a meal. Once we had been a large community of men, women, and children. Now all we needed were two or three pots.

We sat silently, as if we grasped for the first time that we were the remnants of a large camp, part of which had scattered and part of which had died strange deaths. The late Fingerhut used to say that the convoy was the figment of a sick mind; he would also say that a thief's end is jail.

As we were sitting there our fiddler appeared, as if rising from the depths. He stood at a bit of a distance, the fiddle in his hand, as if he were afraid to draw near.

"Shmuel Yosef!" called Sruel.

On hearing this, Shmuel Yosef moved to the side. Now everyone got up and wanted to go over to him, but it was just this reaction that terrified Shmuel Yosef, and he ducked down. Then it was decided that only my teacher, Old Avraham, would approach him. But when my teacher did so, his presence must have unnerved the fiddler, and he fled.

About an hour later, Shmuel Yosef emerged from his hiding place, came over to us, and sat down alongside one of the wagons. Only now did we see how worn out he was; his shoulders drooped and a bitter expression hung on the corners of his mouth.

"What happened?" asked Sruel.

"Nothing."

"And where are the others?"

"I don't know."

People did not bother him further, and he sat where he was without moving. Suddenly he opened his mouth and said, "I didn't want to run away. They forced me to. I had it good here." No one reacted to what he said, so he added, "If you don't want me, I'll take off. I'm not blaming anyone."

On hearing this, Sruel went over to him and said, "What are you talking about, Shmuel Yosef, we love you just as you are. You were our fiddler and you'll always be our fiddler. We love your playing and we wouldn't trade it for anyone else's playing."

Shmuel Yosef raised his head and opened his eyes wide, wondering if his ears were not deceiving him.

"You mustn't worry," continued Sruel. "You'll play and we'll see to everything else."

"And you forgive me?" he asked in a choked voice.

"Why do we need to forgive you? Have you done us any wrong? You only brought us good things."

Shmuel Yosef lowered his head and his faded baldness revealed everything that his face couldn't express: embarrassment and contrition.

That night we experienced a closeness that we had not felt for months. Conversation flowed from every corner; people drank coffee and reminisced. Even Itcheh Meir, whose thief's mark was carved on his forehead, disclosed to us something about his compulsion that greatly moved us. Finally, Shmuel Yosef was asked to play; he agreed and stood up. There was great excitement, and when he was finished everyone went over to him and embraced him.

44

The next day no one stirred. Tzilla put up a full pot of excellent coffee and people sat and drank silently. The joy of the previous night had receded; it was impossible to patch together a conversation from what remained. We were afraid to leave the place. The feeling was that were we to move, people would disperse and we would never find them again.

"This is a good observation point," Sruel said, "and we should watch and wait. There's no hurry, and we must regain our strength." Even he, who had been so eager to reach the harbor, did not hurry now. But it was Tzilla's cooking, more than anything else, that kept us tethered to that deserted strip of the shore. Shimkeh and Chiyuk improved the stove and collected driftwood, and Tzilla set to cooking and baking with the diligence of a seasoned chef. The winter sun hung low and pale, and at night we would make bonfires that radiated light and warmth.

The epidemic had greatly weakened our herald, Reb Pinchas. Only here did he begin to rally, and something of his old expression returned. In contrast to the rest of us, he had lost his appetite. Tzilla would make him gruel with honey, promising that the honey would heal him, that there was no remedy better than honey.

It turned out that Pinchas had been harboring a plan to collect a large group of people who would travel throughout the Jewish Diaspora, from city to village and from village to city, to give heart to the weak and the oppressed and to instill faith within them.

"And what of the Redemption?" Sruel asked.

"We'll travel to Jerusalem and from there we'll draw strength. As we say, '*From out of Zion will go forth the Torah, and the word of the Lord from Jerusalem.*' "

"I don't understand you," said Sruel. "We'll leave Jerusalem?"

"We won't leave her forever. We'll fulfill the verse *From out of Zion will go forth the Torah* literally, with a large group that will include a choir and a trio of musicians. We'll prepare everyone in Jerusalem. When the choir is ready, we'll go forth and travel throughout the Diaspora, which is full of darkness and sadness and is in need of a little happiness. At the end of each tour, we'll return to Jerusalem, until we have saved them all. Doesn't this make sense?"

"But we haven't yet reached Jerusalem," Sruel insisted.

Pinchas has greatly changed, although it seems to me that he is still pale. His plan is full of details and sounds logical enough, but there is something about him that's not right. Perhaps I am mistaken. Perhaps my own fearfulness prevents me from seeing things as they are. Menachem asked Pinchas if he could join the choir, and Pinchas promised him that his place in the choir was assured because he had proved himself more than once. On hearing Pinchas's answer, a smile of relief spread across Menachem's face. Pinchas's plans frighten me. People with great visions always have tremendous plans. Dealers are also visionaries, but in the end they turn visions into commodities. And where are they now, those knights of tobacco and salt?

I curled up under the tarpaulin, but I couldn't sleep a wink. Since the epidemic I haven't touched my notebook. Many have abandoned us and many have passed away, and there is no trace of them in the notebook. I pray with all my heart that Old Ya'akov will not be too angry at me. My teacher, too, does not rest. Again and again he entreats Sruel to go back to the place where those in the convoy who died were given a hasty burial.

"A Jew who isn't given a Jewish burial suffers greatly. It is our obligation to arrange for this and to do right by him," my teacher pleads. Shimkeh and Chiyuk are brought before him again. Once again, they swear like peasants that, apart from Bronscha, not a single person from the convoy died in that dreadful place, and that Bronscha was given a Jewish burial in a village called Lutznitz. My teacher hears their testimony with his eyes closed. The eyes of murderers are unclean, and it is forbidden to gaze into them. My heart also tells me that they're not revealing the whole truth, but how can we prove they are lying? They were the only witnesses to our sickness, and only they saw what happened there.

Meanwhile, the wagon drivers have returned to their evil ways. When they get drunk, they force Shmuel Yosef to play for them. Shmuel Yosef does not argue or refuse, but a plaintive sobbing rises from his taut strings.

"Why don't you play some cheerful Jewish tunes for us?" Shimkeh asked, but Shmuel Yosef was so immersed in his playing that he did not hear him. In his drunkenness, Chiyuk poured a pail of kerosene onto the bonfire and almost set the wagons on fire. People tried to prevent him from doing it, but he overpowered them and poured. The flames leaped to great heights, and soot rained down on us.

"You've ruined our nice bonfire!" someone said, but Chi-yuk ignored him. He was staggeringly drunk, and it was fortunate that he had no revolver within reach. Sensing danger, Sruel had hidden it from him, and so we were spared a dreadful tragedy that night.

45

Then it began to rain fiercely, and we were forced to abandon the place. The distance to the harbor was not great, but we were mired in mud. The wagons got stuck in it, and every few feet we had to get out and push them. By the afternoon we had managed to pull ourselves out of the muck and drop anchor in the streets alongside the harbor. Now we were in the very heart of the port, in the midst of the hustle and bustle, being jostled from place to place amid a huge crowd. I had previously been in big cities, but I had never seen such a crush as this. People were almost trampled under the horses' hooves.

After hours of jostling, we were tossed into a crowded forecourt that was full of wagons. I say "tossed," but this isn't the truth. A tall, sturdy man suddenly appeared, shouted, "Follow me!" and carved out a path for us. It was obvious that this man ruled the mob and that they would do whatever he said. His help, of course, wasn't free. He immediately demanded his fee, and it was steep. Had all the wagon drivers been with us, we wouldn't have paid what we did. Only three of them remained: Shimkeh, Chiyuk, and Sruel. Although they protected us heroically, they couldn't stand up against the threats of this thug. It soon became clear to us that he was the leader of a large gang and had scores of thugs behind him.

And this did not end the hardships in Galacz. That night, our wagons were beset by creatures of the darkness who took the form of aggressive beggars, the bitterly disabled, and, most painful of all, child-demons who would thrust their frail hands into our wagons, snatching whatever they could.

It was obvious that here the strong ruled, and whoever wasn't strong would not survive. Chiyuk fired a few shots into the air, but this threat was effective for only a short time.

Toward morning, during the last hours of darkness, there was another attack. This time Ephraim's blankets were stolen from him. The wagon drivers had fallen into a deep sleep and Ephraim's shouts did not reach their ears.

My teacher, Old Avraham, recovered and hurried us to prayer. The overcrowding, the filth, and the violence did not bring him to his knees. He was sure that if we were strict about saying our prayers, we would leave the place as new people. One needed only to purify oneself and refine one's thoughts. The main thing was not to despair, because despair was rooted in impurity. I was afraid of his confidence and of his eyes, where traces of sickness still flickered.

Suddenly I saw a vision of the Prut as I had never seen it before: absolutely clear all the way down to the riverbed. Early in the morning, before the first glimmer of sunrise, the old men would ritually immerse themselves in its flowing waters. And as they returned to the wagons, they would hum the prayer "Lord of the World" in a melody that seared us with its longing.

Since the old men disappeared, it was as if their blessing was no longer upon us. The darkness of morning continues until noon and the low clouds choke us. Who knows what has become of our old men? Sometimes I think that they have returned to their beloved Prut and are sitting on its banks and immersing their gaze in its clear waters. When the hour for prayer arrives, they rise and pray.

Meanwhile, Sruel had made his way over to the port authorities, where boat tickets were sold. We saw him struggling with the door. Since the old men slipped away during the epidemic, Sruel takes charge of everything for us. My teacher and his good friend Yosef Haim hardly ever leave their wagon. My teacher rarely leaves because all our money is sewn into his coat, and Yosef Haim doesn't leave because he is blind. Tzilla stands by the stove and cooks. I've noticed how very focused her expression is: when she cuts the red cabbage she purses her lips like someone trying to prevent his hidden life from emerging.

The convoy is on its last legs. In my dream last night, I saw our flutist and drummer hiding in the reeds.

"Why don't you come back? Shmuel Yosef is waiting for you. We are all waiting for you," I called out as I struggled against a feeling of suffocation. When they heard my voice, they crouched down low.

I tried to get to my feet to go over to them.

"We've already run away," they called out toward me.

"You can come back," I told them. "Everyone loves you."

"We want to go back to the Prut."

"There's no one there; we're all here."

"We'll stay in the reeds; we like the reeds."

"The reeds are damp, and they'll be even damper in the autumn," I said.

"It doesn't matter." They fixed their eyes upon me with complete indifference.

In the evening Sruel came back from the bursar's office with despair in his eyes: there was not enough money for the tickets.

"And if we sell everything?"

"Even that won't be enough."

"Aren't there Jews here?" my teacher asked with a naïveté that touched the heart.

"There are Jews, but they're just the middlemen."

"How much do we need?"

"A lot."

That night Shimkeh and Chiyuk had no pity on the thieves; they beat them until they bled. My teacher begged them to take pity on the thieves, but his entreaties went unheeded. In the end, they caught a young thief, and to their surprise he started to beg for his life in our language. He was swarthy and did not look Jewish. Shimkeh deemed it necessary to give him a talking-to.

"Who taught you how to steal?"

"My father," the thief answered, trembling.

"Stealing is forbidden," said Shimkeh, and released him.

In the middle of the night, Shimkeh and Chiyuk disappeared. Their departure reminded me of other times when they had disappeared. When the convoy ran into hardship—and it happened more than once—Shimkeh and Chiyuk, together with Ploosh and a few other wagon drivers, would raid warehouses and plunder them.

"Thieves!" the old men would shout, and they would refuse to eat from what had been brought. But the other members of the convoy were usually content with the raids because they brought not only provisions but warm clothes as well. They once brought a chest of drawers made of shells, and everyone stared at it as if it were a precious object.

Toward morning, before sunrise, Shimkeh and Chiyuk arrived laden with things and immediately crammed the stolen goods into the wagons. They looked short, bitter, and exhausted. Sruel went over to greet them.

"Was there cash?" he asked.

"No."

"So what was there?"

"Flour and corn."

"And what else?"

"Some clothes."

46

The following day we sold the horses and the remaining wagons. Shimkeh and Chiyuk grumbled loudly, expressing their bitterness in snarls and growls. The buyers were two peasants, a father and son, who paid most of the sum in cash and the rest in provisions. We sold our things to them separately, for a few coins. Among them were the long stoves that Sruel had soldered in Sadagora, the huge pots that we had bought from the gypsies, floor mats, and two carved chests in which the dealers had hidden their wares. That was all we had. My heart tightened at the sight of our belongings. Tzilla asked if it was worthwhile to keep the small stoves, and Sruel made a gesture of dismissal with his right hand, as if to say, "What for?"

To spite us, the peasants took their time loading the wagons, examining every item, joking, and asking questions about their quality. Sruel also gave them his two dogs and asked that they be treated as house dogs. On hearing his request, one of the peasants chuckled and said, "They're already old and they don't bark."

"They have lots of experience. A thief wouldn't dare approach your house." Sruel spoke to them in a pompous tone of voice.

"We'll try them out."

"Trust me," said Sruel, laying his hand on his heart.

The wagons had not yet left, and through the cracks I could see the belongings that had surrounded me since my childhood. I had in the past parted with many of my possessions, but now I saw up close the silent, sold objects strewn about as if they had been abandoned, and I knew that only in the World of Truth would I see them again.

The peasants finally set out, but I remained standing there. My teacher, Old Avraham, stood beside the small Holy Ark and stared anxiously at it.

"We don't have anything now," said Shimkeh.

"We do. We have the money to buy ourselves tickets," Sruel cried out in a vigorous voice.

Tzilla made cheese-and-egg sandwiches and gave one to each of us. Her hands were reddened from the dampness. Over the past few days she had made us three meals a day. When I offered to help her, she said, "I can manage by myself." She was intent on her work and kept carefully to the exact mealtimes. People were very happy with her food, which brought to mind forgotten childhoods and warm homes. When I looked at her, I imagined that I was looking at my mother's face.

Meanwhile, Sruel's falcon appeared in the skies. We could see him gliding silently in wide circles. This marvel, repeated every evening, always stirred us anew. Would he also cross the sea with us? Sruel shrugged, as if to say, *Who knows?* His bond with this winged creature is a hidden one. If anyone asks about the falcon, he says, "Who can fathom the heart of a falcon?"

Without a roof over our heads, we were forced to rent two rooms. The rooms—sort of an annex to a tavern—were narrow and dark, and they were filled with a suffocating stench of beer and vodka.

"Well, that's that," said Shimkeh, and one of Ploosh's expressions glittered in his eyes.

That night, Shimkeh, Chiyuk, and Sruel sat and counted the cash. We had a sum in hand, but not the amount that we needed. Shimkeh and Chiyuk announced that they were prepared to stay behind—that they would work at the port, save their money, and make the journey later. Sruel would not accept their offer.

"We came together and we will set sail together," he said. "We won't leave anyone behind."

For as long as we had the horses and wagons, we had a home. Now, in this godforsaken hostel, with its mildewed walls and sealed windows, we felt like smugglers. The hostel owner would come every day to collect the rent, and it was clear that he, too, had a gang to protect him. Night after night, Shimkeh and Chiyuk would set out on their raids, bringing back full sacks. The next day we would sell the stolen goods. The thought that we were saving up money lessened the humiliation but not the fear.

My teacher said that this was not ordinary suffering, but suffering for a higher purpose. Eventually, he said, it would elevate us. We must not despair. Since the epidemic, we no longer studied Torah and there was no prayer group. My teacher, who had been equally strict in his observance of simple and difficult laws, who had always spoken to the heart of the matter, now talked in incomprehensible verses. One had to assume that he did not know about Shimkeh and Chiyuk's nightly wrongdoings. Had he known, he would certainly have been alarmed. His eyes have dimmed, but his mouth and his heart are still close to the Torah, and it is the sole subject of his thoughts.

From the time that we sold the remaining wagons and horses, it was as if the dreaded Ploosh were once again dwelling among us. I see his expressions in Shimkeh and

Chiyuk. They now blame Sruel for selling our home too hastily. Sruel explains to them time and again that this money will not be squandered; we'll guard it closely and buy the tickets with it. The word "tickets" echoes in my ear like a whispered charm. But Sruel's explanations do not satisfy them.

"Instead of a house," they say, "we've been left with a moldy kennel."

"I don't understand you," says Sruel, as if he were facing a fortress wall instead of two people.

To alleviate their sadness, Shimkeh and Chiyuk have bought a few bottles of cognac, some cheese, and some pickles. They sit on the ground, eating and drinking, playing cards, and cursing the Jewish merchants who fortify their doors with iron bars and lock them tightly. The gentiles' shops are easier to break into, but they don't contain merchandise of any value. The previous evening, despite all the fortifications, they broke into a Jewish shop and found plenty of clothes. Sruel greeted them happily afterward and called them men of valor. Blind Menachem constantly asks how things are, how everything is progressing. His curiosity is insatiable. Sruel invents things that never happened to tell him.

When his mood was improved by the cognac, Shimkeh turned to Shmuel Yosef, the fiddler.

"What wrong did we do to your friends that they ran away?" he asked. "Didn't we provide them with a living?"

"I don't know," said Shmuel Yosef, springing up fearfully.

Shimkeh must have forgotten that the wagon drivers had often woken the musicians during the night and forced them to play. At first the musicians would refuse or argue, but eventually they learned that if they did not give in to the wagon drivers' demands, the outcome would be grim. It was true that in moments of grace—mainly when they were drunk—the wagon drivers would give each of the musicians a bar of halvah. And sometimes the musicians received even more generous gifts. But most of the time the wagon drivers ignored them, as if they were servants of lowly status.

"We spoiled you too much," said Shimkeh.

Shmuel Yosef was terrified by his threatening words.

"You're right," he said.

"If the deserters return, we won't accept them. They betrayed our trust," said Shimkeh.

I wondered at the expression he used—"betrayed our trust"—until I remembered that the wagon drivers had frequently used those words. It must have been a phrase that was used by people in jail.

Shimkeh did not let up. "Where did you intend to run off to?"

"Not far."

"And you weren't afraid?"

"We were afraid."

"And why did you run away?"

"I didn't want to run away," said Shmuel Yosef, as he shrank into himself.

Again I saw the musicians before my eyes. There was a wondrous harmony in their playing, as if they were all born of the same father. At the end of a night of playing they would sit together silently on the ground. After an hour of silence, one of them would say, "Time to go to sleep." They would immediately get up and drag themselves over to their wagon. No one spoke to them. Their lives were shaped by the notes of their music, and when their music fell silent, it was as if they had ceased to exist. Many knew Shmuel Yosef's story of terror, but no one knew a thing about the flutist and the drummer. They were inward-looking people and only rarely, if things became unbearable, would they complain.

"I was sure that they wouldn't run away," said Sruel.

"It's a fact, they ran away," said Shimkeh.

"I find it hard to understand."

"We spoiled them too much."

"I miss them."

"I can get along fine without their noise."

"If I knew where they were, I would go and bring them back."

"I'm not prepared to forgive them."

"Why not?"

"Because they betrayed our trust; a person shouldn't desert his post."

"In spite of this I would take them back."

"I wouldn't. Where we were, anyone who betrayed a trust would have been murdered."

"It's strange," said Sruel, "I can't fall asleep anymore without music. I have insomnia."

And for a moment it seemed to me that it was not about the flutist or the drummer that he was talking, but about some part of his body that had become detached from him. Until he found it, his life would not be worth living.

47

Our lives now took on a different rhythm. We would get up late and trudge slowly over to the kiosk. Its owner would make us coffee, and we would pay him with some provisions. Every morning there was haggling and quarreling. From the kiosk, we would head toward the docks and the ticket office. Sruel bought an old wheelbarrow, padded it, and put Ephraim in it. Ephraim is as happy as a child.

Blind Menachem's eye sockets appear to shrink. "What will be?" he asks.

Every night Shimkeh and Chiyuk carry out their raids on stores and warehouses, but they have not yet come back with cash. We sell the stolen merchandise, but at the end of the day, there isn't much left to save. Then Shimkeh and Chiyuk decided to take Itcheh Meir with them. Itcheh Meir refused, claiming that he was weak and did not have the strength to break into stores. Shimkeh and Chiyuk did not stand on ceremony.

"For years you stole like a lion," they said, "and now, when we need to buy tickets, you claim that you're weak."

Itcheh Meir was shocked by the directness of their allegation. "I didn't steal," he said.

"So who stole if not you?"

"I don't know."

"If that's the case—take it from us, you stole."

"I gave back everything I took."

"Not everything."

Shimkeh and Chiyuk then forced him to accompany them on their raids, and Itcheh Meir had no choice.

"What are we doing here?" asked Tzilla unexpectedly. Since we sold the wagons, Tzilla has undergone a frightening change. Her face has suddenly become gaunt. For years she was quiet and withdrawn, but now her eyes dart about angrily, and every few minutes she utters a fragmentary sentence or a string of broken words. It's hard to understand the source of her fury. Sometimes it seems to me that she blames the people who fled the convoy. Her bearing is tense and her actions are abrupt. I'm afraid of her movements; it's as if she's about to draw a knife from the lining of her coat and stab one of us. My teacher, who always treated her with respect, approached her. Tzilla lowered her gaze and said nothing.

"What's the matter, Tzilla?" asked my teacher as he bent his head toward her.

"A crime."

"What crime are you talking about?"

"Our crime."

"How have we sinned?"

"Theft."

On hearing this word, spoken with restrained fury, my teacher lifted his hands and said, "Tzilla, my dear, there are so few of us."

"He is the one who gives."

"About what theft do you speak?"

"Sir," she said in a dry voice as she turned toward him, "don't you see anything?"

"See what?"

"Since we sold the wagons we've turned into thieves."

"Tzilla," said my teacher, "your words make me afraid."

Most of the day we stand on the dock and try to guess what the next day will bring us. The waterfront is threatening: violent people swarm about in every corner, and the local Jews keep their distance from us. At noon we make our way north toward the enclave where fish are sold. We immediately light a bonfire and roast some fish. Tzilla no longer takes part in preparing the meals.

At times it seems to me that this is nothing but a bad dream. In a little while we'll return to our wagons and to the waters of the Prut. Indeed, from every alley familiar faces leap out. Last night, I saw in a corner a woman huddled in a blanket, muttering fiercely and trembling. I was sure that it was Mamshe. When I called out, "Mamshe!" she gave me a venomous glance and I fled.

My teacher, Old Avraham, now urges me on in a strange way. He keeps telling me that in these impure places a Jew must stick his head in a book. If he is referring to pimps, they are indeed all over the place, and prostitutes stand on the main streets. Thieves lie in wait behind fences, and whenever an old man passes by, they attack and rob him. The dockworkers and sailors abuse any woman they come across with curses and lewd gestures.

We return in the evening and shut ourselves away in the hostel. Shimkeh and Chiyuk sleep next to the door, Sruel by the window, and Tzilla sleeps in the smaller room, which is actually a storeroom. Since we sold the wagons, Ephraim again fills our nights with dread. My teacher sleeps next to him, and whenever he wakes up shouting, my teacher whispers in his ear, "Dreams have no meaning," and lays his hand on Ephraim's forehead.

Night after night, Shimkeh and Chiyuk set out on their raids of the stores and warehouses. Last night, they were very bitter and claimed that they should be getting a cut from the merchandise they were bringing, to buy themselves sausages and vodka. Without real food, who has the strength to get up every night? Sruel did not try to bargain with them, and just gave in. With great embarrassment, they thanked him. Itcheh Meir goes with them. At the outset his successes were infrequent, but in the past few days he has managed to bring back some cash. Shimkeh and Chiyuk saw him in action and marveled at his nimbleness. They treat him like a real partner now and share their drinks. But even now he doesn't look like a thief. His mannerisms are as steady as those of a dealer. It's hard to understand what he's hiding. Now he's content, as if his embarrassing secret had been given a clandestine remedy.

The *Gregorius* is the name that appears on the fluttering poster. The ship's bursar has written up an invoice on a piece of cardboard and given it to Sruel. Now I see him up close: he's of average height, clean-shaven, and he's wearing a striped suit and a beret.

"In the entire port there's no other ship you can trust," he said. "Only the *Gregorius.* The rest are nothing but scrap metal; no one should entrust himself to scrap metal. Furthermore, the captain is German, as are his officers. They are disciplined professionals. That's what I can offer you."

"We're three hundred short." Sruel revealed our secret to him.

"Go to the Jews; they help their brethren," said the bursar.

"Where are they?"

"Everywhere."

Sruel made a strange gesture, bending over as if he were

bowing, and said, "Thank you very much, sir. We will do everything within our power. When does the ship sail?"

"Tomorrow."

"Ah, so we must hurry."

"Correct."

When Sruel returned to us, he was as white as a sheet.

We went back to the deserted waterfront and sat down. The skies were overcast and brown seagulls circled above us with wild cries. Years ago, we had been attacked by hornets in an open field. Sruel had not been afraid, and he got rid of them as if by magic. I wondered why he was not now making the same nimble movements to drive away the malevolent seagulls. He just sat where he was and stared at them as if he had been bewitched. The words that more than once had saved us from despair were nowhere to be found. In vain did my teacher attempt to embrace us all with his pleading glances. It seemed as though we would sit there until the seagulls pecked out our eyes.

Fortunately for us, a fisherman appeared and offered us fresh fish. Sruel went over to him and bought some for all of us.

"Where are you coming from and for where are you bound?" the fisherman asked.

"For Jerusalem."

"Almighty God," said the fisherman, and he crossed himself. The awe in the gaze of this gentile surprised us all. Without our asking, he also gave us bread and hard-boiled eggs.

After the meal, my teacher cried out, "We must condemn despair!" We immediately rose to our feet. Slowly, listlessly, we walked along the seashore. Ephraim no longer prophesizes. He asks questions, and there is an alarmed tone to them. Sruel pushed the wheelbarrow and explained that now it's up to us to raise the money, no matter how. The phrase "no matter how" frightens me, perhaps because my teacher once told me that it's forbidden to say "no matter how." Since we sold the wagons, Ephraim stopped speaking of the future and retreated to visions of the past, to the years we spent together. Longing draws his heart to the Prut. When he speaks of it, the brightness returns to his eyes. But Sruel dampened his enthusiasm.

"Even then the prayer shawl was not woven of pure threads," he said.

It grew dark, and we returned to the hostel and lit a lamp. Sruel opened two bottles of cognac, filled some shot glasses, and invited us to drink with him. After he had a few, he was in high spirits. He embraced Shimkeh and Chiyuk and referred to them as brothers in great deeds. He also drew Itcheh Meir close to him and said, "We have great hopes for you, comrade." Itcheh Meir joined in the drinking and looked content.

"So, how do you do it, Itcheh Meir?" Shimkeh asked in a tone that held a trace of mockery.

"I don't know," said Itcheh Meir, and he shrugged his shoulders.

"Don't play the innocent."

"My word of honor!"

"And you didn't learn from anyone?"

"No."

"So when did you pick it up?"

"In childhood."

As soon as Itcheh Meir said the word "childhood," his face reddened.

Sruel kept drinking and went from one person to the next, filling everyone with hope and encouragement, saying that although the amount of money we were short was large, we would get it in the end. Shimkeh and Chiyuk would do their best, and Itcheh Meir would not drag his feet, either. Sruel was in high spirits, but his voice was not the one we were used to, and this frightened us.

While Sruel was downing drink after drink, piling up lofty words, envisioning miracles and wonders, Itcheh Meir put on his jacket and said, "I'm going out."

"Where to, comrade?" Sruel sought to detain him.

"To make up the shortfall."

"But carefully, my friend."

"I promise."

"We know that you're a person of great resourcefulness. But still, be careful." Sruel spoke with a kind of brotherly gentleness. As soon as Itcheh Meir went on his way, a heavy gloom gripped all of us, as if we had turned him in. Shimkeh and Chiyuk quickly got drunk, babbling and poking fun, and plotting all kinds of strange settling of scores with the wagon drivers who had fled. They even mentioned the departed Ploosh. Sruel asked them not to raise specters of the dead, but they continued to fault Ploosh, calling him a swamp creature and a troublemaker.

Later on, they also went out. Sruel asked them to do everything with caution and not to endanger themselves unnecessarily, because we still faced great trials. Shimkeh and Chiyuk were confused. Barely in control of themselves, they shouted at the top of their lungs, "Death to thieves and freedom to the tormented!"

Sruel accompanied them part of the way. Pinchas the herald, who let something foolish slip from his mouth, was sternly upbraided by Sruel.

"Shut your mouth!" Sruel shouted at him. "People are going forth to war, and you're slandering them. They're endangering their souls, and you're calling them vulgar. Where do you get the nerve? Bow your head and sanctify their names." My teacher, who feared a quarrel, placed himself between them.

"Children, what do you want from me?" he cried. "I'm old and weak."

After that, all words died out. Only Sruel continued to mutter. He confused things that had taken place years ago with what had happened the previous night, grieved over the two musicians we had lost, recalled the pitiable Mamshe, and praised Shimkeh and Chiyuk, who had always been at the forefront of the camp. A short time later, his spirits fell and he burst into tears. He wept for his father and his mother who had to wander about in their old age, who visited him in jail every month, bringing provisions and clothes. He cried bitterly, and no one dared to approach him.

Two hours later, Shimkeh and Chiyuk returned empty-handed. It turned out that sturdy guards had been posted at the doorways of the stores and warehouses. Two thieves were beaten before their very eyes, and they had not been able to break in anywhere because everything had been sealed with iron bars. They looked dejected and embarrassed, like soldiers who had failed at their mission and expected to be reprimanded.

"If that's how things are, we'll need to find another method," said Sruel, without blaming them at all.

But Itcheh Meir, it turned out, had been more fortunate. He returned with his pockets full of coins. Not that his luck was complete: one of the beggars from whose pocket he had stolen woke up, pulled out a knife, and stabbed him in the arm. After his wound was washed and dressed he was given a sandwich, and Sruel sat and counted the coins. Most of them were base-metal coins that are usually given to beggars.

"How much is there all together?" asked Itcheh Meir.

"There's some, but not much."

"It won't be enough."

"No."

230 / Aharon Appelfeld

. . .

Toward morning, at the last watch, Sruel decided by himself that there was no choice but to steal Yosef Haim's money. The blind old man had sewn his money into the lining of his coat and we knew that he had a treasure trove in there, but we had no idea how large it was. It would have been preferable to send Itcheh Meir to perform this delicate task, but Sruel decided that he must do it himself. As he would sometimes say, there are tasks that a man must do with his own hands. It was his misfortune that Yosef Haim woke up and began to scream at the top of his lungs. On hearing his shouts, the owner of the hostel came running. Sruel hastened to explain to him that two thieves had just attacked the old man and robbed him of his money. They had been armed, so there was no point in putting up a fight. The owner of the hostel listened, spat to the side, and said, "Thieves, criminals—they're everywhere!"

It turned out that we had not been wrong; the money that was in the lining of Yosef Haim's coat made up the shortfall.

Early in the morning, without stopping to drink coffee at the kiosk, we headed straight for the docks. Itcheh Meir and Sruel sat for a long time in the bursar's office. They gave him the banknotes and the coins that they had accumulated in small envelopes. The bursar counted, counted again, and eventually issued the tickets.

On their return, no one greeted them. The sun came out from behind the clouds and lit up the quays. Porters dragged bags and brown seagulls circled above, shrieking with hunger. In my mind's eye, I again saw Yosef Haim's thrashing legs as Sruel was picking apart his coat. He had struggled with all his might to rescue his savings.

Then everyone got busy preparing their bundles. It was strange that this activity, which was completely without grace, brought to mind the clear waters of the Prut and the willows along its banks. It appeared to me that all those who had fled were standing at some distance and staring at us. I was surprised at Sruel for not calling out to them.

A little later, Sruel did speak. He spoke of the sea, calling it the Great Sea. His hands were pressed close to his body, like a man who does not ask for thanks for what he has done. Everyone listened very carefully. Yosef Haim no longer cried over the robbery. But his eye sockets were as swollen and red as if his eyes had just been plucked out.